The Curvature Of An Absence

Jorge Armenteros

SPUYTEN DUYVIL

New York City

"Absence, the highest form of presence."

—James Joyce

PART ONE

Chapter One

Where there was water, there is nothing but sand; a desert that extends far into the horizon. The sea has disappeared; the only blue there to see is the one from the sky that looks down on this improbable absence. Without waves, all I hear is a silence as vast and profound as the sea that is no longer.

I turn my back on the empty seabed and enter the day that grows in front of me, naïve as if nothing extraordinary has ensued. The day is correct so far; nothing remarkable has occurred except that I have been engulfed by the unanimous silence of a sea-abandoned shore.

With every step I take, the sounds begin to burst into my reality until I come to stand in the midst of this regular day in the heart of the hustle and bustle of my village. Once surrounded by the expected, a sense of serenity enters my consciousness. However, a particular taste, sour perhaps, of the immense silence remains in my mouth.

I decide to stop at a corner café and pretend to be at ease with myself. I order an expresso and drink it at once. Again, the sour taste, but no silence. On the contrary, I hear a mélange of voices, noises, and glasses clinking. The sound of smoke spirals away from the cigarette a young woman dangles from the corner of her mouth—the natural sound of things.

On one of the walls, a picture hangs, ignored. It depicts the sea in all its magnificence, embracing the shore of this village of mine. A past that nobody here seems concerned about. They drink their coffee, smoke their cigarettes, and carry on with their lives as if the sea was still there. As if the sea was still there…

I then overhear the young woman with the cigarette asking directions to the beach. She appears to be in a hurry and insists on getting there by the shortest route. The man who answers says that there is no beach in this village, that she should give up on the idea of finding one. She thanks him for the information and walks away from the café opposite where the sea used to be. She walks slowly, no longer in a hurry, it seems.

To extend my right to linger unmolested, I order a glass of pastis and continue to observe the people that come in and out of the café. Nobody addresses me directly with their words; with their eyes, however, I am questioned. I turn my eyes away from the eyes that turn my way. I do not want them to discover that my eyes have just seen an absence I cannot explain. I must keep quiet about that vision, as quiet as the silence that vision provoked.

As the minutes go by, I confirm that this day contains enough ordinariness to be as mundane as any other day. There is no apparent need for alarm or desperation. There is no reason for celebration either. The world around me turns on its axis as it always has. The absence of the sea, then, must be a personal tragedy. This, an idea I feel inclined to reject, for I am such an unimportant person to be presented with such a magnanimous occurrence. And, in addition, I am all alone.

Perhaps the best thing to do is forget about the presence or absence of the sea and focus on the sour taste of the silence I experienced. However, what I now taste in my mouth is not sour but the pastis' licorice root, cardamom, and rosemary flavors. With no point of reference to guide my inquiry, I decide to set aside all efforts to comprehend what I saw this morning. I am just another man drinking pastis at a corner café.

Once I decide to leave the café, I am confronted with

various options. I could wander aimlessly just for the pleasure of having no aim. I could return to my apartment and find reassurance in what is known and expected. I could also go back to the shore and challenge the veracity of the vision I saw earlier. This last option has the capacity to deepen my uneasiness, so I discard it immediately. Seeking reassurance, I then make my way to my apartment and find it exactly where it should be.

All objects inside the apartment are just where I left them this morning. Nothing is missing; there are no absences. I have returned in my entirety; nothing of me has gone astray. As I look out the window, I confirm that all adjacent buildings are where I left them this morning. I would love to have a view of the sea from this window! I could keep an eye on its return. But I am not that lucky. Or perhaps I am. Hard to say.

Inside a dusty shoebox, I find my collection of old photographs, the ones I have ignored for so long. Why bother with the past if the present is burning with urgency? Except that, this time, the urgency points to the past. Since the photographs are in no order, it is difficult to find what I want. But it does not matter; what I need are images of my sea, regardless of who is posing or for what reason the photograph was taken. I want to regard that which is now absent.

I find several pictures where the sea is prominent. I need to evaluate if the sea ever revealed signs of wanting to vanish. I do not care for the tides; their movements are predictable and modest. I care for significant changes in the shoreline, pulling the great mass of water toward the horizon.

Considering the seasonal changes, the vagaries of the wind, the occasional storms, and even the moon's phases, not a single picture reveals a fugitive sea. It has always been there, the sea, hugging the shoreline. It is impossible to conceive of any of these pictures without the sea. If the sea were absent, the pictures would not have been taken at all, and my friends and family would not have visited me either. In whose company did they want to be? Mine or that of the vast body of water? I know the answer.

Perhaps the best is to let this day continue its course without further considerations. Not knowing is only a beginning. The problem is that I do not know what it is that I do not know. I saw the vision of an absence. That is a lot to wonder about. And after all, wondering is the first of all the passions.

#

On this new and delicate morning, the path leads me to the shoreline. I hope to dispel the disappearance of the sea as an erratic vision of yesterday. In vain, for what I confront once more is sand and more sand. If the sea were to return, it must come from far away. I try listening for an early wave, hoping to confirm its arrival: nothing, only silence. I should refrain from invoking its name for fear the sea would rescind its advance and spurn this shore. A mercurial sea this is, as fickle as it is vast.

How long an absence? One day, or one hundred days, or one hundred years? I cannot tell. Even the seagulls are desperate; I can see it on their faces.

I still have myself. My body and my mind are intact. Nothing has abandoned me. My life continues regardless of the vacuum left behind by the sea. I can choose to act as if the world has come to an end. I can also choose to regard the absence as a condition to endure and an illness to bear.

The immensity of this silence, however, is without parallel. Never have I encountered such a voluminous and ethereal space. I cannot touch it, nor can I measure it. It is both within me and around me. I felt it yesterday as well as today when standing in front of the empty seabed. Yet, it did not accompany me to my apartment. It did not sleep with me. I wonder if this silence owes its existence to the absence of the sea. Would the existence of one exclude the existence of the other?

I stand firm and close my eyes. I try to attenuate all sensorial perceptions. I try to turn down the volume of my thoughts. My attention is exclusively directed to the sounds my ears are capable of capturing. I hear nothing, nothing—an unpolluted and sideral silence. Afraid I may fall deep into such a vast void, I open my eyes and start walking away from the shoreline.

I return to the center of the village, where Zotikos waits for me at Café Central. Immersed in a book, he does not acknowledge my arrival. He appears calm as if nothing unusual has ravaged this day. I wonder if he knows what happened to the sea. He will most likely deny having any knowledge even if he were aware. I see that he is back to reading poetry, Neruda. That will give him a good reason to speak tangentially. If I were to relate what I just experienced, he would regard it as a fictional account. Not different from how we regard any other daily event. We do not recognize a solid line between fiction and reality. Why should we?

Since he has yet to do so, I go ahead and order two glasses of pastis. I would do just as Zotikos and dive deep into the words if I had a book with me. Not because I want to drown my sense of uneasiness, but because I need to find some answers. Everything that has yet to happen has already been written about. And there are entire libraries to safeguard our future. But when a book is not available, there is pastis at hand.

We remain seated in front of each other without speaking a single word. Zotikos reads Neruda's political verses while I sip pastis and think about an abysmal silence. Not speaking to another human being is a kind of silence. But that is not the silence of a void, of an absence. What I experience now in front of Zotikos is the lack of verbal communication. This is not silence. This is an agreed form of sharing. Agreed, because we each know what the other is doing and accept it as a valid form of exchange.

It then occurs that Zotikos looks up from his book and takes the opportunity to drink some of his pastis. He regards me with attention, and I can tell that he ignores what worries me at this moment. He asks me if I ever feel tired of just being a man. I tell him that I only dream to rest among rocks and wool. He smiles and goes back to reading his book. I wonder if he would miss the sea as much as I already do. Would his life change much if the sea were never to return? Would he even realize the immense body of water has vanished? I ponder for a while before I finally decide to interrupt his reading.

—What's Neruda up to?

—Saving himself and the world, I assume.

—He was gloomy at times.

—He had no option.

—Probably not… I wonder what was missing in his life.

—Neither fame nor women, that's clear.

—He needed the sea. Do you need the sea?

—I don't know, I never lived far from it.

—What if the sea abandoned you?

—Women have abandoned me recently.

—That's not the same.

I refrain from pursuing this line of questions. Clearly, Zotikos has not approached the seashore in the last couple of days. If he has, then the abandonment by Laura weighs more than the abandonment by the sea. Perhaps he feels Laura is permanently gone while the sea has no choice but to return at some point. This, of course, is a conjecture of mine.

Could it be possible that Zotikos experienced an immense silence when Laura left him? Maybe that silence still lingers inside his mind and makes him this quiet, unusually quiet. He will not speak about such feelings in a direct way. Instead, he will twist all logical and causal events and render a contorted explanation sparing him from saying what he really feels.

—When Laura left, was it all quiet?

—You know, Neruda had twenty love poems and a song of despair.

—Did you hear that song?

—I only heard when she said goodbye.

—And what did you hear after that?

—Poems, many of them, in all languages. Can you

hear them?

—No, I don't hear anything.

Zotikos reads those poems for a reason. He certainly appreciates the artistry of Neruda's words. But most likely, he is trying to formulate his own poem. He must be juggling all those images and sentiments and weaving them into his personal poem. He is not simply reading Neruda; he is creating alongside the poet. A writer only begins a book. A reader finishes it.

If I were to ask him if he wants to write a poem, he would probably say that such an exercise is a waste of time. He would certainly deny the need to massage one's emotions. He may even say that his life is about to come to an end. Or he would argue against the topic in some other way. And because I am not exactly sure what he would say, I pose the question.

—Do you want to write a poem?

—What's a poem?

—That which you're now reading.

—I'm just looking at the words.

—What about the images and feelings those words invoke?

—That's for Neruda to figure out.

—Aren't you curious?

—I'm very curious.

—So, what's the meaning of the words?

—I would have to think like Neruda to know what he felt when he wrote down these words.

—But what do the words mean to you?

—I would have to write them down myself to explore their meaning.

—So, then, you do want to write a poem.

—What's a poem.

—A poem is when the silence within speaks out.

—Is there a silence within you?

I could answer that question but decide to stay quiet for a minute. Zotikos does not expect an answer. He seems content to sip a little pastis and return to reading his book. He knows that I will continue thinking about the question and eventually present my answer. He also knows that I may not do so today, that it may take multiple meetings like this one for the answer to surface. No argument is ever finalized, and no certitudes are ever agreed upon. We only traverse the tortuous course of interminable exchanges.

Zotikos is astute enough to sense there is something

of consequence brewing inside my mind. His question about my inner silence is by no means naïve. He does not know the nature of my consternation, but I am uncertain about it myself. First, there is the absence of the sea, unexplained. Then, the evisceration of all sounds at the shore. I believe this is the order of events. However, the vacuum created by an immense silence could have drawn me to the shore, where I then witnessed the terrible abandonment. That is possible as well. But the order of factors does not alter the product. Both experiences are devastating.

I finish the glass of pastis while remaining my quiet self. The morning has exhausted all its possibilities. There is still the afternoon and perhaps an evening to gallop through. And then there are the questions. Without asking, I take the book of poems from Zotikos' hands. He seems happy to let it go and reaches for his glass of pastis. With the book under my arm, I walk away into my silence.

#

I better not be asked where I have been, for the answer will not suffice. I better not be interrogated about the deaths of the day, for there have been too many. I better be left alone to unravel the meaning of what I have lost and what I have discovered. If I seem tired, it is because momentous happenings weigh me down. And all I can do is act like a quiet dove and lower my head.

I could ponder what has rained on me for the rest of the day. Yes, I could try to find a logical system to explain the unexplainable. But to what avail? Neruda wrote that he did not want "so many misfortunes" for himself. Neither do I. So, I will refrain from mentioning that which is absent for fear that it will become a memory. And because the essence of a memory is its absence, I will not let it crystallize as such. I could refer to the sea as the "crib of all waves" or the "blue above the sand." I could also forget what may have been lost and revel in the newly discovered silence.

I can conceive of a silence that always existed. Like the one before the earth came to be. That fluid where all the galaxies now float in a sort of dormancy. That universal silence must be the primary matter of all existence. Therefore, it must be part of each of us and probably percolates all occurrences. The vastness of the blue above the sand is such that once it became absent, the resulting vacuum came to be filled by the ubiquitous primary silence. Perhaps that is why I heard it at the shore. Precisely where the exchange took place. If, indeed, that is what happened.

I decide to distract myself by reading Neruda's book. I should know better, I know… But the moment requests liberation. Unintentionally, I come across a poem entitled "The Great [blue above the sand, or crib of all waters]." Speaking directly to such entity, Neruda writes in one of the verses: *Your energy seems to slip away without ever being exhausted, it seems to circle back into your calm.* After reading the poem with maximal attention, I come to understand that the blue above the sand could not simply slip away, that it is probably circling back into its original calm, into its primary silence. As a result, I begin to consider the extraordinary events of the last couple of days not as misfortunes but as a luxuriant offering.

I step out on the balcony of my apartment and watch as the evening begins to flood the streets. The daily cycle reminds us how human we are and, thus, how vulnerable. I feel somewhat calmer since I know not to ponder much as it begins to get dark. I welcome the breeze, dry, a little jagged. I hear some words and music far away. The night is itself an offering to which I yield from time to time.

Descending on the streets emancipates my corralled concerns. There is freedom to be had. The wind knows about it, and so do a great many people who make the night their stage. They all gather, young and old, around the numerous venues dispensing freedom. In the absence of natural light, what we see is the result of intention. We shine light and unveil. We turn the lights off, and the veil hides what is there for real. This interplay of revelations and hidings makes a masquer-ade of the night—a perfect justification for not wanting to know.

I meander through the streets expecting nothing. Unimportant as I am, people pass by me with ease. I am fluid and inconsequential. This, a much-beloved free-dom I seek. Soon enough, I reach the shoreline with its sentinel lampposts shining an amber light. The light travels perhaps a mere fifty meters before it gives its life away, opening an ample space to the darkness beyond.

Illuminated by the light, the seabed exposes its dry and naked belly. The crib of all waves has yet to return.

From where I stand, I can see the neon lights of a few establishments where the mass of people continues to frolic with abandon. But I cannot hear their voices, nor can I hear the music. I feel the wind swirling around my body, but I do not hear its whisper. Even the seagulls are quiet. The large and majestic silence is what I hear. The absence of the blue above the sand once again materializes in the form of silence. I look around me in hopes of finding someone else with whom to talk. But there is nobody. I am alone within this silence in front of this dark absence. I then fill my lungs with air and call the crib of all waves as loud as I can, "Where have you gone?" The words fall out of my mouth without making any sound. It is as if they have been expunged by the phenomenal silence.

I came out into the night looking for freedom and expecting very little. Instead, I find myself alone, with no voice, facing this magnanimous void I cannot understand. Perhaps the offering to be had is the precious amber light that falls on my skin. I had not considered it as a gift. It is kind; it does not oppose; it molds around my body. And if I were to block it with the palm of my hand, the light would not feel rejected. It would please me to bring this light with me wherever I go. But the light resides at the shoreline where it will remain. It does not need me. An unnoticed miracle this light is.

I leave the silence and the amber light behind and walk back toward the crowd, where I immerse myself in the noises and the voices. The angular shadows cross my path at every step. I am aware that I am going through the thickness of the abundant night. But I am of no consequence, and the night does not know about me.

CHAPTER TWO

She frequents the open market not because of the abundance or freshness of products but because of the aromas saturating the air. She described her sensorial adventures while having a glass of pastis with Zotikos and myself. Clearly, her desire is not to buy any vegetables or fish at the market; she desires to smell them. I first thought she was a sensualist, and I later confirmed she was one. Laura does not seem to care for the object itself but for how the object unchains a sensorial experience.

If she left Zotikos, which she did, it must have been because he did not exude an aroma worthy of her sensitivity. Perhaps Zotikos does not exude the right pheromones. Perhaps Zotikos has a stale and musty smell. He does spend a fair amount of time with books, and that may contribute to the problem. The truth is that I never saw them physically close to each other. They were together but apart at the same time as if a miasmatic ravine existed between them.

I was not expecting to come across her on this clear morning. I only wanted to buy a few vegetables and return to my apartment to reconsider the meaning of silence. But as I reach for succulent heirloom tomatoes at my favorite stand, our hands get entangled in the same gesture. As I look up, her eyes meet mine, and I feel exposed. I then place the tomatoes in my basket while she brings hers close to her nose and savors their sweet aroma.

—These are sweet creatures.

—Yes, Laura, they seem to be. Have you tasted them?

—I don't need to. I don't want to. I just want to smell them.

—How does the rest of the morning smell to you?

—Like any other morning. Except that the sweetness of these tomatoes makes it a little rounder.

—Is this what you expected, or are you missing any other smell this morning?

—Why do you ask? Smells are never absent; they are always around you. You must pay attention.

—Can you smell the… You know, at the shore, that blue above the sand?

—You must be referring to the sea, are you?

—I don't really know what I'm referring to. But are you missing any smell this morning?

—What seems to be missing is the saltpeter in the air.

—Is it not there for you?

—No, it seems to be absent.

Laura turns away from me and becomes absent herself. She may not want me to ask about Zotikos. She may not want to talk about the smell of the crib of all waves. She may fear I will make her feel uncomfortable. And without saying another word, Laura vanishes among the crowd. For a moment, I feel like going after her to ask about olfactory absences. What does that feel like? But I do not go after her. I do not want to feel like Zotikos, abandoned and in need of poetry.

People in the market are as agitated as usual. Modern savagery: when obtaining your alimentary subsistence requires screaming, haggling, and thrashing around. The one emotion lacking in the tumultuous morning is fear. Most people seem fearless, engrossed in their quest for vegetables and parts of dead animals. Nobody would suspect this village has just experienced a devastating loss. Or, perhaps, because their sense of stability has been shaken, they pour such vicious energy into procuring their basic need for food.

I try to stay in the periphery of the market, only diving into the crowd when I see an ebb of people at the stands I frequent. Why would I expose myself to bodily contact? Why would I risk engaging in casual conversation? If someone were to ask me how I am doing today, I would have to lie and tell them that this is a day like any other. They would probably sense a certain strangeness in my answer. How would I hide my sense of bewilderment, my uneasiness about what I have seen with my own eyes? No, I better avoid people for the moment.

On the way to my apartment, I will pass by Café Central. It is inevitable. Too early for Zotikos; he will not be there. It is also too early for me to start worrying about what he may say or ask. I know he will ask me to return his book. But I am not finished with that book yet. Not that I want to read it entirely, but Neruda had something of relevance to say. All a coincidence, most likely, but there may be more of those coincidences hidden in that book. Or perhaps there are no coincidences at all; I may be finding that which I want to find.

Café Central is virtually empty. I hover over our usual table, trying to capture that stale and musty

smell Zotikos seems to exude. I do not perceive anything other than the smell of cigarette smoke from a
nearby table. I do feel a certain degree of absence, however. But given the fact that Zotikos is not here, that is
to be expected. I wait a couple of minutes to allow for
unnoticed miracles to occur. There is nothing. There
is no sense in scrutinizing what this place is all about
when we are not here. So, I take my leave and continue
walking toward my apartment.

The seagulls fly above my head in large circles. They
seem anxious. They must be wondering where all the
fish have gone. The absence of the blue above the sand
must be devastating for them. Perhaps there are dead
fish lying exposed and rotting on the seabed far into
the horizon. Or maybe the mass of water took everything with it when it retreated from the shore, leaving a
clean, deserted expanse of nothingness. These seagulls
are not birds of prey, but they would probably behave
like the people at the market in the absence of their
food source. I better take cover.

As soon as I get into my apartment, I reach for Neruda's book. I do not exactly know what it is that I am
looking for. I am ready to accept the meaning of any

verse, even if the verse appears completely unrelated to my current situation. All I can say is that something went missing and something else appeared. I do not know if those events were purposely conjured by a force as powerful as that of a poet. Maybe the chasm provoked by the absence of the crib of all waves is a poetic one. Maybe I just fell from the edge of a verse and landed on the verse below, one that has no sound.

I read a few verses in silence and wait for the powerful force to strike me. I then read out loud and wait for brutal coincidences to emerge. Nothing happens. I may be reading with pointless intention. After placing the book aside, I go out on the balcony and try to imagine how Neruda would have read those verses with his own voice. Old poets had a cadence; I have heard some of them. But perhaps the poet does not want to impose his own sound; he would have wanted for my voice to impart a personal sound and meaning. After all, the literary work is something like an arena in which the reader and author participate in a game of the imagination.

I fetch the book and bring it out to the balcony. My hand flips through the pages and stops at a random point. As loud as I can, I start reading a verse in the middle of the page. Neruda says that "Like a long absence, like a sudden bell, the [blue above the sand] doles out the sound of the heart." And here again, he pierces my reality with his words. Could it be that the universal silence at the shore is nothing other than the sound of my heart? If so, how come I have never heard it before? Was I not listening? As for the absence, I am not strong enough to consider the possibilities. Sometimes we find what we are looking for. Other times, what we are not looking for will find us.

With haste, I close the book and go back into the apartment. The rest of the day promises a path of reconciliation with my own self. My mind will not be quiet until I attain some mastery over the propositions made by Neruda. True, what he makes are mere suggestions. But once the mind gets a hold of those, a disquieting wind is unleashed. I bring to the kitchen all the vegetables and the fish I got in the market. There they will remain until I am ready to deal with material matters. What is urgent now is to find quiescence of the mind. With the book under my arm, I cross the threshold of my apartment, of my unrest. I throw myself out into the world again.

#

Relative to the weight of the emotional turmoil in this book, the object itself is surprisingly light, not even a pound of paper and ink. What really unsettles our mind is completely incorporeal. Fear has no weight of its own, neither does happiness. And the grand sentiment of love, ancient and leaden, floats in the air like a feather.

Without wind to push me forward, I walk at a very slow pace and wait for the day to soothe my unquiet mind. I walk as if I do not know where I am going. To the passersby, I may seem to be shuffling slowly toward nowhere. That is my corporeal self, the flesh that people can see. Inside my mind, the thoughts move at a different rhythm, albeit syncopated, but with direction and purpose.

I turn all the necessary corners until finally arriving at Café Central. Everything is in its proper place at this time of the day, including Zotikos, who is at our usual table pretending not to be waiting for me. I take all the necessary steps until I come up to the table and take a seat. Zotikos does not look up from the book he is reading, a different book whose title I cannot see from this angle. In the spirit of parallelism, I open Neruda's book and start reading as well.

My eyes walk through the words, those incorporeal markings on the white page, until a verse shakes me up. Neruda writes: *Were you to ask me where I've been/I would have to say, There comes a time.* It so happens that a time has come, even though I am not sure of what it really entails. And that is the problem, that I have entered a certain awareness I have yet to understand.

I close the book and signal the waiter. Mauricio knows not to ask for what I want but to proceed with bringing a glass of pastis on ice and a carafe of cold water. That is exactly what he does. I pour a little water on the pastis and take a small sip of the cloudy liquid. I am now ready to address Zotikos.

—As you can see, I brought back your book.

—You could've kept it longer.

—Is dangerous, this book.

—In what way?

—In the way that only a book can be dangerous.

—You mean, it made you think.

—No, I was already thinking. But it seems Neruda must have pondered some of the same thoughts.

—And what's dangerous about that?

—Well… apparently, he found some answers. In my case, I have yet to find one.

—So, the danger resides in the possibility of finding an answer. If you find what you're looking for, then you would have to deal with it.

—I wasn't looking for her, but I found her by accident this morning.

—What answer was that?

—Laura.

—She's not really an answer; she's more of a question.

—So, my question for you is, do you feel her absence?

—There's nothing to feel; she's no longer with me.

—Then, what occupies the space of her words? Is it silence?

—I really don't know how to recognize silence. In my world, sounds populate every corner.

—Have you been to the shore in the last couple of

days?

—The shore is where I'm at. This is the very edge for me.

—Fine. What's there beyond the edge?

—I'm too busy with this book to entertain other concerns. Everything that matters is now happening within the pages of this book.

—Can I see what you're reading?

—If you promise not to take it away from me.

—I won't.

Zotikos hands me the book he is reading. The cover contains a self-portrait of Egon Schiele, where the painter is posing with a Chinese lantern and fruits. He looks sideways at the observer, a rather intense and difficult gaze to endure. Below the painting, I finally see the title, *The Notebooks of Malte Laurids Brigge* by Rilke. This confirms that Zotikos is going through a period of existential disquiet, even if he refuses to admit so. I refrain from opening the book to prevent any unexpected encounters.

—What's happening in this book?

—Nothing and everything, and that's the good fortune.

—Does it take you beyond the edge?

—I don't know yet. I suppose it will.

—And what would you do if there's a silence beyond the edge?

Zotikos does not respond to my question. He seems bothered. He attempts to calm himself by looking away into the emptiness. Then he breaks the silence.

—What did Laura have to say?

—Are you trying to fill the silence with her words?

—No, I'm trying to make her absence disappear.

—She spoke about the saltpeter in the air and how she misses that.

Abruptly, Zotikos snatches the book out of my hands and immerses himself in the pages. Without looking up at me, he takes a sip from his glass where the ice has already melted, and the pastis is probably warm. I take a sip myself and prepare for the difficult work of handling Zotikos' mood. Sometimes it is better to hover over the issues and not bring down Zotikos' walls. If I show respect for him, he will do likewise.

According to him, nothing and everything happens in that book. He recognizes the brilliancy of such stratagem. The measure of a book should be estimated as a ratio; that is, the extent of the concept achieved in relation to the economy of events presented. But how to measure the emotional effect of a book? It gets complicated. Zotikos may be looking for emotional support in the book. But at the same time, he may be looking for nothingness. To know how the words, the phrases, and the images in this book impact Zotikos' condition, I would have to be Zotikos myself and have undergone the same misfortunes. The book that Rilke and Zotikos are writing together belongs only to the two of them.

The answers must exist somewhere. The world has turned for enough centuries to have spun all possible answers to all possible questions. Considering the innumerable books written in all languages, I imagine most of those answers have been written down already. However, I have never read about the absence of the crib of all waves. And I assume that Zotikos has not found the soothing he seeks in Rilke's book or any other book. These are personal misfortunes. Perhaps there are tangential approximations that may impersonate as answers, written by Homer or by any other author after him. But I would not know where to find them. We may need to do our own unveiling; we may need to tear down the walls ourselves.

Would it be possible to read, think, explore, share, write and cry, all at the same time? Let me not forget hope. Would I be able to hope for an answer in the process of doing all the above? Let me not forget life. Would I be able to live in the hopes of finding answers in everything I read, explore, think about, share, and potentially write, even if it makes me cry? Would I be able to do it alone? Unthinkable, we all have doppelgängers. Besides, books are not written alone; they are written in the company of the universe.

Once I see a softening in Zotikos' facial features, I decide to interrupt him. First, by raising my glass of pastis and gesturing for him to do the same. Then by toasting to our new venture.

—I want to toast to our book... cheers!

—All of your books belong to me, and all of mine belongs to the two of us. But which one are you referring to?

—The one we're about to write in parallel.

—I have no knowledge of that book.

—Neither do I.

—Perfect, cheers to the unknown book.

—Now, we must give birth to it.

—The book doesn't exist, correct?

—No, it doesn't exist yet.

—Cheers again! To the nonexistent book.

I do not say another word. The cheering contributes very little to Zotikos' mood, and he goes back to his reading and internal sulking. But I know the currents in his mind are circulating around the idea I vaguely proposed. He will return to the concept of the parallel book from some oblique angle. He will see the beauty in creating something out of nothing, transforming the sense of absence into a presence. I will not mention the book again until it begins to emerge. It will take form just like any other creature, by the accumulation of our souls.

The air remains light this afternoon. Maurice knows to bring another glass of pastis when the first one fades away. In peace this very moment, I let time take its time and enjoy the small silence around me. Nothing like the silence at the shore; that one needs to be written about.

#

The first consideration pertains to the degree of universality. If I were to write about an absence, would it be an absence experienced only by myself? Or possibly one shared by the entire human race? Should that absence be revealed to the reader *a priori* before she tackles the book for the first time? Does Zotikos need to know what absence I may be referring to? Does it matter if the absence is untouchable, fluid, and evanescent as if it were absent itself? I have no answer for these considerations. And these being only the first out of many other considerations to entertain, I better try to resolve them. So, I take to the streets, determined to ascertain the sentiment of people about the vanished body of water.

The shore will have to wait. I am not starting there, for the experience will likely unsettle me. I need peace of mind and stillness. I need to flow among people, unnoticed like a ghost, and alert nobody. Listening will be better than talking. I can think as much as I want, provided I do not think out loud.

I decide to start at the market. Here nobody cares about anybody else, and people say and do what they want—a somewhat organized mayhem. All customers share one need, stock up on something fresh according to their wants. The sellers, after much screaming, look already tired by noontime. With ease, I infiltrate the crow. I listen to the loose conversations, to the whispers, and the request for a kilo of rhubarb. I watch hands exchanging money. I pay close attention to people's faces, to their expressions. I soak myself in the fluid humanity of the market. And here I rest until reaching the conclusion that an absence is not in people's minds. But could it be that the blue above the sand is not important to them? The absence of fresh fish may be more important than the absence of the medium where the fishes swim. Who am I to judge?

Leaving the market behind, I continue walking until I reach my favorite park, where the shades assume a bluish color and the wind parades absentmindedly: fewer people, greater peace... perhaps more sincerity. On a bench sits an old man reading the paper and smoking. I approach the bench and sit alongside the man. I do not have today's paper, nor do I smoke, so I do not have much to share with this old man. However, I find the precise moment when he looks up from the paper to ask him a question.

—Anything interesting happening in the world?

—All sorts of things. The world is crazy.

—Have you met him?

—Who?

—The world.

—Yes, I have. I've known him for a long time. Believe me; he's crazy.

—But crazy in what way?

—You can read it for yourself. Just two days ago, an old man like me was walking his dog on the beach. Nobody knows what happened, but he disappeared together with his dog. They're both still missing.

—Do you go to the beach often?

—Who, me? No, not me. The world is crazy, you know.

The old man throws the cigarette butt on the ground and crushes it with his shoe. He folds the paper and tucks it under his arm. He walks away from the bench, mumbling something I cannot understand.

The world cannot be crazy, as this man said. The world has no mind of its own. Incongruous and absurd things can happen in this world, but that does not make the world crazy. I prefer the word "insane" because it implies the opposite of sanity. Again, the word suggests an absence, the absence of sanity. But in the case of insanity, the absence of what we consider sane ushers another state with remarkable attributes. Insanity does not resemble a void or a vacuum; to the contrary, it could be rather flamboyant, irritating, even dangerous.

I am careful not to walk too close to the shore. I must remain inland enough so that there is no possibility of seeing the absence of the crib of all waves when looking down the street. I would rather not confront that tragedy at this moment. Sufficiently safe, I keep my course until reaching the shop where I usually buy the pastis I consume in my apartment. Casiv is here, ready to talk about the French Fifth Republic. Casiv is a man of convictions. He seems as content as usual, and nothing on his face reveals urgency. So, I take the risk of asking.

—How's today different from yesterday?

—There's no difference; I'm still breathing.

—But do you have enough air?

—All the air I want. Look, it's even free.

—And what would happen if someone sucked away

all the air?

—That's why I have gills, just in case.

—But those gills don't work here on land.

—No problem, the sea is a short walk from here.

—Yes, the blue above the sand... Have you been there recently?

—No, I haven't had the need to use my gills.

—I went there yesterday, and it wasn't the same.

—How was it different?

—There was something missing; an immense body wasn't there.

—What sort of body is that?

—The body that extends itself beyond the horizon.

—I cannot look that far. Were you able to breathe?

—Yes, I was able to breathe perfectly fine, but there was this overwhelming silence. Something I've never experienced before.

—If there was silence, then there was no air. You must have been asphyxiating. You need gills like the ones I have.

—What if I couldn't have submerged myself? What if the crib of all waves wasn't there?

—What if today was different from yesterday?

—It may, or it may not be. I really don't know. That's what I'm trying to find out.

Casiv turns away from me to pay attention to a customer who just entered the shop. I take advantage of this moment of distraction to exit the shop without saying goodbye. Out in the open street, I feel cast aside, as if the world were intent on denying me confirmation. But this is not the moment for self-deprecation; this is the moment for finding out how flowers bloom.

As I walk around, I confront the solidity of this day. The houses stand where they should, and so do the trees. And nowhere do I find a fountain crying as if a larger body of water had abandoned them unexpectedly. The village lives the life of the village, unaffected, not necessarily content, but not in misery either.

I let go of the bridles and follow my own steps. They know where to go, my steps. They ignore the conundrums of the mind and follow their own rhythm. A syncopated rhythm that, seemingly confused, knows how to anticipate. The anticipation being the early arrival at Café Central before Zotikos has had the chance to put a stake on our table. So, I proceed to do just that. Here I now sit, trying to bring my mind to rest.

The fact that, thus far, I have failed to confirm a perceived absence does not imply the absence of such an absence. I must be gentle with myself and allow for human error. I may need to let the obtuse circumstances emerge on their own, without provocation, without squeezing them out of the reality of the day. Clearly, people do not seem to be molested. On the contrary, they seem oblivious to the fact that life has changed in a significant way. Just knowing that people's nature is not one of complacency, I must conclude that they honestly ignore the gravity of the absence. Or even a more disturbing proposition: they are aware of the absence but care not about it.

The wind blows softly, making the dry leaves spiral shamelessly. And with the same abandonment, Zotikos arrives and sits in front of me. He carries a book with him which he places on top of the table as if it were an offering. Without greeting me, he makes eye contact with Maurice to request our respective glasses of pastis. Then he turns toward me and does not say a single word. I know he has a lot to say; that is precisely why he is silent. Once again, in the spirit of parallelism, I remain quiet and wait for the pastis to arrive.

The book is entitled *The Savage Detectives* by Bolaño. This is clearly a dangerous book, one that makes you think about the universe. I gave this book to Zotikos a while back, but we have never discussed it. I contemplate the book. It sits there like a brick, heavy with all those words. It proposes and taunts; it probably laughs at us, as it laughs at itself. That is the kind of book this is.

Zotikos has the ability to suggest something without using words. Perhaps that ability only works when the audience, me in this case, can understand someone else's silence. Once again, it is the accumulation of the soul of each other that brings us together in silent understanding. And for that very reason, I know he will not talk about *The Savage Detectives*. Zotikos is in acquiescence with my proposal of a joint literary venture, but he will never say so in plain words.

I grab the disjointed book and search for a phrase that could explain our project. None of the passages I read serve the purpose well. I know Bolaño talks about catastrophes, those in the past and those yet to come. But, in this instant, I do not come across anything that resembles our most recent absence. And perhaps the problem resides in thinking that the absence is indeed a shared one. It is entirely possible that I am the only person experiencing such an absence—a disturbing thought, that is.

I place the book down on the table and sip a little pastis. I wait for Zotikos to have some pastis himself. Then we both regard each other, knowing that we are about to begin something we do not really understand. I trust that Zotikos is prepared to rise to the challenge. And Zotikos himself must be counting on me to illuminate the mysteries we have yet to bespeak. And after a few minutes of quietude, I break the silence.

—Are you afraid?

—Not more than you. Are you afraid?

—I'm only afraid of not finding any answers. What if we give birth to a book that fails to contain an answer?

—Are we giving birth to a book, the two of us?

—You know we are. That's why you brought Bolaño's book.

—Yes, I thought it was pertinent. But I'm not so sure what we are writing about.

—That will become evident as we each start writing our part of the book.

—The only thing that's evident to me is that nothing is evident.

—Let's then begin with non-evidence. For example, is this day any different from any other day? Is there any evidence to support that a cataclysm has come upon us? If not, then this day is a perfect starting point.

—It was not evident to me that I would be writing this book until you proposed it yesterday. As of today, it is not clear to me why I should do so.

—Exquisite, the evidence is absent.

—But was it ever there? Did we ever have a clear and transparent reason for pursuing this endeavor?

—We don't know what may or may not have been there. All we know is that there's an absence.

—Yes, there's an absence. And maybe there're multiple absences. How could we define the essence of an absence?

—I don't have an answer. That's why we must write this book.

Chapter Three

To search for evidence feels a lot like sweeping the sidewalks after a street fair. You brush all sorts of debris into the gutter until a reasonable amount is amassed. Then you pick up all discarded matter and dump it in a trash can. In the process of moving all that garbage, traces of evidence could be found. Clearly, what we are looking for is not bound to be easily accessible. It must be dug from the filth. A dirty job this is, and it does not smell very good either.

Should I look for evidence through the trash of my past? Should I turn over those stones under which there is rotten flesh and desiccated dreams? I may discover that there was never any blue over the sand at the shore. My memory tells me otherwise. But why would I trust my memory when it is nothing other than another absence, the absence of reality lived a while back and no longer available. The evidence of an absence is a confirmation of the past. Looking for evidence feels like looking for the past within the past. How likely would it be for me to succeed in that endeavor?

I put aside those considerations and step out onto

the balcony. From this point of view, I cannot see my past; what I see in front of me is the moment. I know I am losing this moment as I think about it. But it does not matter. That is only a small absence. What matters more is to initiate the process of discovery, to write that book in parallel. And in so doing, I will gain more than what I will be losing. Zotikos will be there as a witness; otherwise, the writing is at risk of disappearing and becoming an absence itself. I cannot take that risk.

I marvel at the sonic presence of the noises coming from the street. By the time my brain registers them, they are already gone. Like the waters of a river, the noises flow and become history only to be replaced by similar noises arising from the same street. What is the evidence that I heard those noises? An imprint on my brain cells? A memory of having heard them? The truth is that there is no evidence.

At moments like this, I need grounding. So I get dressed in haste and descend to the street. I need to find her, Carolina, for all the grounding that she can give me. Where she could be, I do not know. How I could find her at this moment, I do not know that either. But that is how we first found each other, by knowing the other existed but not exactly where. Thus, I walk as if I am not looking for her, knowing that I am expecting to find her. As I walk, the sound of my steps, the people, and the seagulls all compete to leave an imprint on my brain. But all I hear is the small silence of Carolina's voice.

Sometimes she follows me without me knowing, like a chasing leopard. She keeps her distance and avoids revealing herself for an entire afternoon. She then pounces and taps on my shoulder, pretending to have just come across my path. I know she is lying then because there is no immediacy to her regard as if she had already found me hours before. Other times, she does not tap on my shoulder at all; she just follows and observes my movements, my comings, and goings, my errors, without pouncing on me. I do not know how often that happens, but it does happen often. The times that I manage to spot her first and take her by surprise, she becomes startled, and her regard palpitates with immediacy as if the leopard was caught off guard by its prey. But those occasions are rare.

I wish I could smell her and follow her trace. I wish I could hear the sound of her whispers. I wish I had a sense of her intentions for this day. But I do not count on any of those benefits. All there is for me to do is walk and hope for the unannounced miracle of our encounter. Those encounters make her presence more palpable. In between those rendezvous, her presence is of a different substance, less corporeal but just as intense. The truth is, she is never absent, even when she is not there.

Do I need to find Carolina, or do I need her to find me? That may be irrelevant at this point since I have already embarked on this uncertain walk. And if we do come across each other today, would I tell her about the book? If my reason for seeking her this moment is a need for grounding, then why talk about the book, something that does not even exist? Maybe what I need is for her to tell me about her life without me, that aspect that I know nothing about. Or, perhaps I should avoid hearing about my absence because it may be brutally inconsequential. Yes, there is a danger in knowing what our absence feels like.

There is the park ahead, with all those trees guarding the fresh air. And under one of them, on a wooden bench under the shade, Carolina is not sitting. I have found her there before, reading or just dreaming, but not today. Nor is she crossing the bridge that leads into the old part of the village, a suspended place that has offered several meetings before. I walk by the old fountain where several aquatic monsters surround a faun in the midst of blowing his horn. But I do not hear the horn, nor do I hear Carolina's voice. I walk some more in no specific direction with the sole purpose of ushering in the unexpected miracle of an encounter. And with every step I take, I confirm Carolina's absence.

The gravity of the moment is such that I did not realize how close I am coming to the shore, the proverbial straw that broke the camel's back. I do not want to be that camel. I can barely manage one absence at a time. So, I change course at once and make sure I'm heading inland. Besides, I have never met Carolina by walking alongside the crib of all waves. She never seems to be at the edge of anything; she is always central.

And she becomes central to my day when I see her standing at a corner, seemingly waiting for me. There she is, Carolina, dreaming those dreams I never learn about. Walking toward her is like walking into a sun; she burns me, and her light blinds me. I put my hand on her shoulder and feel her presence, a real and hard presence. And so is her voice.

—What took you so long?

—I didn't know you were waiting for me.

—I'm not necessarily waiting for you. I'm just standing here. But I expected you would come by a lot sooner.

—I walked around somewhat.

—I know, I saw you.

—Shall we walk together? Where would you like to go?

—Let's go where the wind will take us.

In between the ethereal wind and the hard land—that is where she resides. But I need grounding today, so I need her to be close to the hard land. She takes my hand and leads the way. We walk for a while without saying a word. Her steps are firm and light at the same time as if she is walking over solid clouds. On her face, I see no trace of concern, of worries. That is all I can unravel. Whether she is happy or not, is always a mystery.

We arrive at the fountain with the monsters and the faun; Carolina comes to a stop and lets go of my hand. She turns to me and regards my face. I feel exposed, naked in front her light, and I close my eyes.

—I saw you walking by this fountain today. You seemed worried.

—I was looking for you.

—You'll never find me that way.

—I know.

—Tell me, what worries you?

—It's immense; it's haunting. But I cannot touch it.

—Then let's not talk about it.

—No, let's talk about a book.

—What book?

—It doesn't exist.

—Perfect, let's talk about that book. What is it about?

—That book talks about that which is not there, about absences.

—You cannot touch that book, neither an absence.

Carolina is right; I cannot touch an absence. Neither could I touch a book that does not exist. She knows very well that agreeing with my precepts provides me relief, that my worried face will be transformed by acquiescence. There is the grounding: when she shares my concerns without having to break them apart.

I could see myself creating a character based on a

few of her idiosyncratic qualities. I could also create a character based on her absence and try to find her that way. Likewise, I could write an entire book and not include her at all, thus, solidifying her absence. But if I were to talk to her about the book before I start writing it, would that alter the destiny of the book? Would her impressions about the nonexistent book force my pen? This moment she is untouchable, and so is the book.

—Carolina, can you imagine opening a book and finding only blank pages? Nothing written on them, not a single word.

—That would be a very difficult book to read. You would never know where the book ends.

—Maybe the book doesn't end.

—If it doesn't have any words, the book cannot have a beginning or an end.

—By not having a single word, the book would contain all the words.

—But the words are not there, correct?

—No, but their absence would be there. I can imagine that absence could speak volumes.

—Have you ever heard an absence speak?

—Yes, I have. By means of pure silence. And a silence so vast and so deep that I was afraid to fall into it and not be able to resurface. Have you ever heard a silence like that?

—A silence like that is not evident to me. But what's evident is that this is an important part of your worries.

Carolina knows how to follow my steps without being noticed. She also follows my thought process like the edge of a shadow. I could shine the light away from my concerns, but the shadow has already been cast. I know she will not scrutinize those worries any further. She has already found them and made me aware that she has. There is the grounding without wreckage.

—I worry sometimes. And then I must go out walking. That doesn't provide the answers, but it feels soothing.

—I know, I often see you.

We leave the fountain and head for the narrow streets of the old village. Once inside the maze of streets and odors, I abandon my need to know exactly where we are. I tell Carolina that I have closed my eyes, that I am following her blindly. She responds by squeezing my hand harder and bringing me closer to her. Like this, we embark on a march that has no beginning and

60

no end. Without words, on the blank page of this afternoon, we walk.

#

I open my eyes. My life shows up right in front of
me. It contains me, but it does not contain Carolina.
There is no use in looking around for her—she could
not be found that way. Our next encounter, if there is
such a thing as a next encounter, will happen on its
own. All I can do right now is to carry on with my day
and hope for enlightenment. Enlightenment, however,
in the sense of discovery and advancement, advancement in the sense of moving forward with the book
about what is not there.

As I look at the buildings around me, I realize I am
not far from Café Central. All I need to do is walk slowly, make a few turns right and left, and soon enough,
I will be at Café Central. Zotikos may, or may not, be
there. What is now urgent is to arrive there and unleash
the writing process. A process that will first happen in
our minds before it finds itself in print. The materiality
of the book is secondary at this point. The meeting of

our minds is what matters now. Zotikos will find every possible way to derail the process, even when he needs it as much as I do.

Walking slowly suits me better; it gives me the opportunity to observe how people behave in the aftermath of such a monumental absence. I come across people, and their dogs, mothers with their infants, pigeons, drunks at the park, the whole of what mankind has to offer in this village, and nowhere do I find a worry or a concern for what is no longer there. Whether this is a travesty or simple slackness of the mind, I do not know. And that is the problem, am I experiencing a dissociative state of mind or a disconnection between people's emotional response and their reality?

Turning left one more time brings me to the street leading into Café Central. I walk slowly for the last few meters until I can see the place in its entirety. From afar, Café Central promises nothing. It is only when I sit at our usual table that the place convokes its force. Once in situ, the mind departs in all directions. Not because the place itself conjures any magic, but because it permits my mind to take flight. Others have blamed the pastis as the igniting force that triggers what ensues.

But that is a limited understanding. The mind always finds a way to expand when nothing is expected.

There he is, Zotikos, ahead of me in presence. Perhaps not so molested by the absence he has incurred, perhaps just waiting for me to share such weight. He seems like a mere mortal from a distance, but nobody could divine his capacity to analyze life and bear its truths. I can see that he has brought yet another book with him. And I can only wonder.

As soon as he sees me approaching the table, Zotikos closes the book and regards me with the intensity of a predator, as if he was waiting for the precise moment to attack. At once, he jumps to his feet and signals Maurice. He then pulls a chair for me and waits there in pure anticipation. When I reach the table, we both sit down without saying a word. We look at each other in silence and remain inside ourselves while in full awareness of the other. What I hear next is the sound of glass as Maurice lays the pastis on the table. Zotikos, then, launches himself into the abyss. He drinks from his glass and starts talking.

—You want us to write a book about nothing. Is that it?

—I want us to write a book about what's not there.

—The book is not there. So, in principle, we could write about the book itself.

—Sure, but that would be too impersonal.

—So, you want to write about yourself.

—No, I want to write about the absence outside of myself.

—Well, is there such a thing as any absence existing outside of the self?

—I'm not sure. And that's part of the problem. If indeed, there's no absence outside of the self, by writing about that very external absence, we would be writing about what's not there.

—I'm content with not being anywhere.

—But you're here right now, and I'm sitting in front of you.

—Then we cannot write about ourselves since you have just confirmed our presence.

Zotikos drinks a little pastis and goes back to reading the book he brought today. He is not only reading; in his mind, he is already fabricating complex stratagems that may have a place in our book. I also suspect he is trying to forget that Laura is no longer with him.

He will not admit to that like he never admits to feeling lonely. Zotikos pretends to come to Café Central for a drink and relaxation, but I know he comes for the slow accumulation of the soul of another. He ultimately wants to satisfy his human need for an exchange with another mind.

—What book are you reading today?

— *Hopscotch* by Cortázar.

—What made you select that book?

—Neruda said that anyone who doesn't read Cortázar is doomed. I don't want to be that unfortunate. Besides, Cortázar seems to be interested in destroying literature.

—But he obviously couldn't. See for yourself; you're reading his book.

—That's proof.

—That's proof that nothing is ever destroyed.

—Transformed… We're all in this world to be transformed, not destroyed.

He does not want to be destroyed. Neither do I. The world will not be destroyed. But if transformation is the natural and expected process, then I need to understand if an absence is finite or if it is only an intermediary stage. Will the blue above the sand transform itself into another material entity, elsewhere, replacing another entity that has, on its own account, also transformed itself into something else? Would an absence be transformed into another absence? That is a dangerous thought.

—What happened to Laura?

—Do we have to talk about that?

—We don't have to talk about her. We don't have to talk at all.

—That's what I was expecting.

—You're lying.

—What makes you believe I'm lying?

—Because you come here to this table to drink your pastis and to sit in front of me.

—I thought we were supposed to write a book in parallel.

—We're already writing a book, the two of us.

—And when was it that we started writing that book?

—A long time ago, even before we met each other. We started writing it as we were reading the books of so many other authors. You're not reading Cortázar by chance, nor were you reading Neruda by chance either, or any other author for that matter. You're looking for your own book in theirs.

—Then I'll know what happened to Laura when I finish writing my part of the book.

—That's fair.

Zotikos never asks me about Carolina, nor do I tell him much about her. He knows that she does not live with me and that we see each other from time to time. What he does not know is that those encounters are never pre-arranged. They take place when chance conjures them. Zotikos does not know how it makes me feel when Carolina disappears, when I am left in suspense, not knowing when the next meeting will take place. There is so much we do not tell each other. Nevertheless, I know him well. I know his instincts and some of his fears.

The sky begins to turn gray, and a fresh breeze blows away the napkins on the table. I welcome the imminent rain. I wonder what happens when it rains over the vast extension of sand at the shore. Does the sand yearn for the humidity it has lost or does the sand pretend not to care? It is irrelevant for no amount of rain could ever restore the blue above the sand.

Slowly, at first, the water begins to fall from the sky. I am happy because it may bring some relief or at least a memory of previous wetness. Then there is thunder, and the sky turns darker. Zotikos seems to ignore the changes around him and continues to read. He may be trying to drown the storm's noise, the one outside and the one inside his mind. His lips, interestingly, are moving as if he is reading and needs to pronounce the words to bring them into being.

—Why don't you read out loud?

—I'm already reading out loud.

—I cannot hear you.

—Because you're listening to the rain falling.

—Are you listening to what you're reading?

—No, it is the voice of Cortázar that I hear. He's wondering why he's writing this very book. He says he has no clear ideas, that everything is looking for a form or a rhythm, that he writes within a rhythm.

—There's a rhythm to the rain falling.

—Are you within that rhythm?

—No, not yet.

I listen to the rhythmic cadence of rain and thunder

and find it utterly present. The rhythm asserts itself and does not ask permission to exist. It is a profound and dark rhythm that reverberates within me. It wants to stay inside of me, different from the intermittent flashes of lightning that live a fugitive life. Regarding lightning, we anticipate its absence the moment it brightens the sky. We know it will only last for a fraction of a second. Then it will be no longer. We harbor such acceptance and suffer not. And that is the kind of acceptance I lack when thinking about the crib of all waves.

For the moment, I continue listening to the forces of nature and try to deepen my understanding of their impact. The magnanimous energy released by every thunderclap will dissipate almost immediately. Still, the reverberations will linger in the form of a rhythm, a rhythm that could influence the writing of our book. The cadence of the prose could emerge from thunder and persist as continuous rain. That may be the persistence needed to write about absences.

Maurice comes by our table, and seeing that our glasses are empty, he goes to fetch for more pastis and ice. He returns and serves both of us without saying a single word. He knows Zotikos will not respond once he is immersed in a book, and all he needs from me is a simple nod. I nod to what is expected, a simple acceptance, that is. But to events that derail the natural order of things, I cannot nod in harmony.

—Zotikos, do you expect the rain will stop?

—The rain has no will of its own. How can you expect it to behave in one way or another?

—I've seen the rain stop many times before.

—I don't expect anything. What's the use in expecting?

—A confirmation...perhaps.

—And what happens if there's no confirmation?

—Then you know your expectation was wrong.

—Isn't that a form of confirmation?

—It is a confirmation, but different from the one you had expected.

—So, what's the fate of the original expectation?

—It ceases to exist.

—Well, but...does it cease to exist altogether, or is it temporarily absent?

—I don't know. That's what I'm trying to understand.

The element of time... I have yet to consider the

temporality of the vast absence. I believe it has existed for a few days. Would it be permanent? And if it were, would the absence cease to exist as an absence and become a presence as real as any other? Like the falling rain, once it has stopped, who could confirm that it was there? The remains of the rain… a puddle on the street, wet clothes on a line, or perhaps the distant reverberation of thunder.

CHAPTER FOUR

Where could she be, Carolina? Perhaps walking on the opposite side of the village, where the hills climb lazily, and people want to think they are different. Or she could be sitting at a terrace while watching the world unfold right in front of her. She is an astute observer, I must admit. Maybe she is still in her apartment pondering if it is the right time to unleash the day. She could also be watching me from an oblique corner while waiting for me to become more and more anxious.

I will assume that she is watching me right now as I stand on this bridge of ours. Taking that into consideration, if she were watching, all my pantomime would be recognizable to her. I will try not to show any signs of anxiety. If she is not watching me, then whatever I do is of no consequence. But how would I know whether she is watching me or not? What I cannot afford is to become rigid and stand on this bridge as a frozen man. I need to be fluid; I need to trust the unexpected.

The river flowing below me must deal with the unexpected elements of this universe, just as I do. The waters of the river flow without asking questions; they just flow. And they will need to confront their own expectations upon reaching the mouth that now opens into a vast and dry emptiness. There will not be a warm reception, the blue above the sand will not be there to embrace the flowing river.

This river existed long before the village did. It has witnessed what sprung up around it. First, on its eastern side, a new village that had become old with the centuries. On the western side, a new village remains new for the moment. The river did not mean to be divisive, its only concern being to flow. Now it finds itself in the middle of two times straddled by this bridge where I now stand. I am sure the river would have taken a different course if it had known its destiny. I do not know my destiny, and the only course I can follow is that of my expectations, even if they prove to be wrong.

I expect that Carolina will come across this bridge at some point this morning. If I remain here, we will encounter each other. Would that be a random encounter? Am I not creating the necessary circumstances for an encounter to take place? Does it matter? The truth is that she does not cross the bridge every morning.

Sometimes she crosses the bridge in the afternoon, and some days she does not cross the bridge at all. Those are the days I find her by the fountain or upon turning an inconsequential corner. Every time that she is not where I think she would have been, I experience her absence. And each absence is different because they occur in different places and at different times. Each time I am missing the same person, Carolina, but there are many shades to her absence.

I start counting the people that cross the bridge. The flow is variable. A couple follows a group of six people, then a lonely man is followed by four schoolgirls, then a loose dog. Their faces mean nothing to me, and I am sure the sentiment is reciprocal. Absorbed as I am in observing the crossings, I do not realize that Carolina is on the other side of the bridge leaning over the handrail while looking down at the river. As comforting as her presence is this very moment, it foretells an upcoming absence. I push that thought out of my mind and walk over to the other side of the bridge. When I tap her on the shoulder, she turns around—she is present.

—It didn't take you that long today.

—I haven't walked too much today. I've been standing here watching the flow of water and people.

—I know, I've been observing you.

—When you watch me from a distance, what do you see?

—I see you.

—Do you ever not see me?

—No, you're always there when I'm looking for you.

—Have I ever been absent?

—Never.

—So, what occupies my space when I'm not present?

—Your space doesn't exist when you're not present; nothing needs to occupy it.

—But imagine for a moment that the river below this bridge has dried out. How would you consider the riverbed?

—There would be no riverbed, only a path.

—What about death? What happens when a person dies?

—There's no death; there's only life.

In moments like this, all I can do is walk. The static mind never finds an answer. It is in the process of moving that the mind finds a way out or in. I take Carolina's hand and walk in the direction of the shore. I am not sure if I have the courage to confront the absence that awaits us there. I am not sure if I would dare to look far into the horizon. I fear a devastating confirmation.

The air seems to get thinner as we march in the direction of the shore. The echo of our steps begins to fade away gradually. All other noises lose their resonance, and a silence begins to grow, engulfing us both. I hold on tightly to Carolina's hand, who seems to be gliding comfortably. My palm is the one wet, not hers.

When we come to the point where a further step would reveal what is there or not, I stop our march abruptly. I cannot imagine what I would do if Carolina were to tell me there is only one blue out on the horizon. She would probably say that the desert in front of her looks majestic. She may not recognize the absence. This is beyond what I can support today. So, I become rigid and search for consolation in Carolina's face.

—What seems to be haunting you?

—A recent memory I can't dislodge from my mind.

—What's the nature of the memory?

—It's completely unnatural, this memory. It's empty.

—You mean to say the memory is a void; it doesn't contain anything?

—No, the memory is intact. The object of the memory is the one that's missing.

—What's the object of the memory?

—I cannot mention it.

—Why not?

—It may affect the object of the memory itself.

—Then just forget about it.

—It's too immense to ignore or forget.

—Then deal with it in your dreams.

Carolina pulls me by the hand and starts running down the street. I follow her and hope she is not heading straight to the shore. She is not; she seems to be making random turns immersing us into the bowels of the village. I could resist this erratic toggle. But why would I reject the apparent randomness of this course when I accept the randomness of our encounters? Or is it that our rendezvous are not random at all? With the last turn she makes, we find ourselves at a dead-end street. She probably knew this street has no exit. She probably wanted us to stand in front of each other with nowhere else to go.

Her breathing is hard, syncopated, but her expression is rather calm. My breathing is calm, but I am certain my expression is more complicated. Carolina looks straight at me, and I wonder if the slight inclination of her head is a sign of pity. Still holding her hand, I absorb her look. I do not know exactly what she sees, but I know she sees something in me. And once she catches her breath, she talks to me.

—As you can see, this street leads nowhere. You can start dreaming now.

—Why would I dream about having nowhere to go?

—No, dream about that immense memory that seems to have a hole at its center.

—I don't want to be cornered by that memory.

—You seem to be cornered already.

—I remember seeing something that is no longer there. And what I remember occupying its place was an immense absence. But you're not concerned about absences because they do not exist for you.

—I'm more concerned about what's in front of me.

—In front of me, I see you, Carolina, and I wonder where we are going.

—So, you have nowhere to go from here.

—I do have a path. I'm trying to follow the only path I know.

—Is it a path of confrontation?

—It is a path of sublimation.

—Then you're trying to fill that memory with fascinations of your own.

—But who else but myself could make sense out of what's missing?

—Anybody else who shares the same experience. You see, I know where the dead ends are, and I know how to exit them.

—Then show me the way.

Carolina lets go of my hand. She offers me a very simple smile. She then turns around and runs away from me in the only possible direction there is—back to where we came from.

#

I knew she would not look back. Once she feels a meaningful exchange has happened, the encounter is over for her. She is free to return to her own world and spin those other realities that exclude me. When Carolina does not see me, I do not exist. There is no permanence to my existence. She does not forget me; she just stops thinking about me for a while. And when she thinks about me again, she manages to find me meandering around the streets of this village. I am certain that each encounter feels fresh to her because she has not experienced my absence. I am alive and present every time she meets me. In between those times, I exist inside a parenthesis.

I do not feel the same way; my yearning is more sustained, and it reaches beyond myself. If the memory of an object is alive, an emotional permanence is guaranteed somewhere inside my mind. The nature of those emotions could be very troubling, some are horrible, and that is the problem. When Carolina walks away from me, her absence is as emotionally powerful as her presence. She continues to exist in full.

I will not follow her down the street. She has shown me the way into this dead end for a reason. Of course, there will be other happenstances at other times. But, for the moment, I need to walk on my own to confront the questions of the day. So, I follow my instincts and direct my steps to Café Central, where a confrontation is always at hand.

When I reach the place, I am surprised not to see

Zotikos at our table. I still occupy my usual chair and signal to Maurice. Café Central does not look the same without the image of Zotikos sitting right in front of me. It feels like a mistake to have the first pastis all alone. It is like entering into a house unannounced, in silence, like a bandit. When Maurice arrives with the pastis, water, and ice, I have a sip at once. This is a time of confrontation.

While waiting for Zotikos, I begin to conceive the structure of the book. It must have a large center, big enough to accommodate all that I have yet to know. If the book is going to incorporate Zotikos' elliptical disquiet, it could not be straight in nature. The book will have to be flexible; it will need to bend at times. Then there is the question of a beginning and an end. If they were to touch each other, the book would have to be circular. Furthermore, if the book is to deal with more than one absence, which is rather likely, the book cannot be hermetic; it will need to be porous and allow inflows and outflows. And even yet, the book will need to deal with its own absence once the reader retires it to a bookshelf and forgets about it forever.

Zotikos turns a corner and comes into the frame

of my reality. He approaches Café Central at a slow and difficult pace as if dragging the entire world behind him. A certain discontent is evident on his face. He must have realized something disagreeable, or he has just started to feel the absence of Laura in his life. Whatever is troubling him, he will try to dismiss the subject. That is his nature. And at such pace, he advances, and I regard his advance.

Once at our table, he sits down and proceeds to say nothing. He does not expect me to say anything either, so I remain quiet. Zotikos irradiates a green anguish, like the faces in the paintings by El Greco. What disturbs him is profound. Maurice brings him a glass of pastis, which he places on the table and walks away without greeting him. He must have understood not to stir the black waters.

As expected, he brings a book with him. Since I do not know what book this is, all I can do is fabricate associations. The book could be about emptiness, perhaps about loss, or even about courage. The book could also be about a book, in which case it would be appropriate because we will speak about our book today. Or perhaps not, we will not speak about a book but about the absence of Laura or nothing at all. But to prevent that last possibility, I part the waters by talking to him.

—Yet again, another book.

—This is a book about nothing. It relates to itself, and it exists only within itself.

—Can I see the title?

—The title won't reveal what the book is about.

—But you just said it was about nothing.

—That's correct, and that's why this book has no title.

—Then it should be entitled, "The Book About Nothing."

—No, it couldn't be called that way. That title would imply that the book is indeed about nothing, creating a strong curiosity on the part of the reader. The reader would want to confirm that the book contains no stories.

—So, what intrigued you about this book?

—I'm not intrigued about the book; I'm intrigued about nothingness.

—Then, I assume you're finding what you're looking for in this book.

—Nothingness is clearly present in the book. But

there's another nothingness outside of the book that worries me.

—What nothingness is that?

—The one surrounding me, day and night, with or without pastis.

—Is it a palpable nothingness?

—It's more like a smell. The smell of something that's no longer there.

—Like saltpeter or like the fragrance of a woman?

—The fragrance of a woman is what's missing, and nothing has come to replace it. Have you experienced something similar?

—I'm missing the smell of saltpeter. The air doesn't seem to carry it anymore.

—And nothing has come to replace it?

—No, not so far.

Zotikos is a man who does not show his wounds. The fact that he acknowledges that something worries him is unusual. Of course, he could not give his worry a form or a face. He gives it the ethereal qualities of a scent, precisely that element that burrows deep into the brain where it leaves a lasting impression. He is missing the scent of a woman; he is missing the woman who exuded that scent; he is missing the presence of that woman. Not only does he face the absence of the woman, but also the absence of the trace of the woman—her scent.

I wonder what absence is deeper. The absence of the object, or the absence of the trace of the object. I suppose the trace of the object still contains a certain presence of what is now missing; it proposes the hope of a reencounter. If I were to walk along the shore and the saltpeter was to engulf my body, would I feel more at ease? Would I gain confidence that the blue above the sand will return to occupy its bed and fill the vast emptiness? And if the seagulls were to return to their flight patterns, to their frolicking ways, would the silence disappear? And if the silence were to disappear, would I miss it? Can silence leave a trace?

Empty-handed, with no clear answers, I prepare to engage with Zotikos in our literary quest. Given his current mood, I expect no cooperation, only tangentiality. But Zotikos is a sensitive man, with a soft core under the hard shield of his intellect. So, when he looks at me as if expecting comprehension, I offer him words.

—The fragrance of a woman is not the woman, but

it represents the woman. When the woman is no longer, the fragrance can take her place. And when the fragrance is no longer in the air, the olfactory sensation stays imbedded in your memory. And when your memories are no longer alive, who cares anymore?

—That's a beautiful sequence of misfortunes. But let's not follow that rabbit into the hole. Today I confront nothingness. I'm not certain that I'll have the same experience tomorrow.

—Then, something will have to come into being to eradicate the nothingness, or you'll have to forget that it exists.

—How can I forget?

—I don't know. It may not be possible.

—So, if nothing materializes soon, I may have to deal with this sensation until it dies away. And once it dies away, I'll have to wait until I forget all about it.

—But you're not powerless, you have the words with you.

—I have the books, but I'm not sure I have the words.

For the first time since we started sharing this table and the venerable pastis, Zotikos dares to express some doubts—those hidden wounds that hurt him now. He places the book he brought with him on the table and looks at me with fragile eyes.

—Here, open the book and look for yourself.

I take the book in my hands, open it, and start turning one page after another. All the words are there, but I cannot tell what they mean.

CHAPTER FIVE

This is where I last saw her, immersed in the aromas of fish, of vegetables, of people. Laura is bound to return to the market; it is inevitable. That inevitability is precisely what keeps Zotikos away from this place. He probably fears a casual and devastating encounter with her, catching him out of words and panting. He is not one to confront the carnal side of his feelings. He prefers to flourish from inside his skull.

I can find Laura because I am not supposed to be looking for her. She does not expect me to be at the market intrigued by her whereabouts. She cares not for me. Different from Carolina, who cares for me and, thus, manipulates her presence. Carolina is not available on my terms and cannot be found. Laura has a different set of terms that do not concern me, so she can be found.

The truth is that I am not looking for her per se but for her impressions. She can sense what I am missing—the crib of all waves—while I can sense what Zotikos is missing—Laura herself. So, if I were to find her, a great knowledge could be had, and a few questions could be answered, provided, of course, that the inevitability of her visit to the market is indeed, inevitable.

I approach the fish vendors to observe the quality of their offerings. A clear eye and a gleaming skin would soothe me. A cloudy eye and a matte skin would confirm my fears: the fish came from somewhere else where there is still a blue over the sand. The clamor of people and vendors is intense. And as I weave myself among them, I come face-to-face with Laura, who greets me with an ample smile. I stop in my tracks and try to hide my shock by speaking.

—You're here! Laura, you're here!

—Not surprising, this is where I find the best aromas. What are you looking for?

—I'm looking for you, believe it or not.

—Then, you found me.

—Yes, I found you. I thought I would.

—Well, now that you found me, what do you want from me?

—Your impressions. I need your impressions.

—My impressions on what?

—What you smell, those aromas in the air.

—Oh, that's simple. Follow me.

Laura leads me through the busy market to a stand
selling spices from all over the world. They have cin-
namon, paprika, cumin, oregano, curry, and exquisite
saffron. With her eyes closed, she seems to be savoring
the olfactory rainbow.

—Do they have salt? I want to smell that.

—Yes, they do.

She points at a bowl containing white crystals and
tells me they come from Thailand. These may not be
coming from the same body of water that I now miss,
but their genre is the same. I take a few crystals and
bring them close to my nose. I then share them with
Laura.

—Here, smell this and tell me what it is.

—This is sea salt.

—Yes, this is the salt that remains after the water
is gone. But there is another salt suspended in the air
that comes from an existing body of water. Saltpeter,
it makes iron rot. When I met you last, you said that it
was missing.

—It's still missing. But why pay attention to that
when there are so many other aromas in the air?

—Because it's the aroma of what's missing, the trace

of the absence.

—What absence are you talking about?

—It's too vast to discuss.

Laura confirms my expectations. There is no body of water suffusing the air with salt. If it was still in existence, Laura would have captured the smell. The wind could not have blown it away. She does not miss the crib of all waves; she does not experience its absence. I wonder whether she is capable of such a feeling—she who is absent herself. Without hesitation, she knows to move on to other scents.

—Now, you need to smell these.

—What do you have there?

—Strong, unadulterated cloves. These are sweet, warm, and woody. If you chew on them, everything opens up.

—Would they make me forget?

—No, they'll make you remember.

—Then I better stay away from those.

Unlike me, Laura is not afraid of memories. Perhaps that is how she moves on through life, through scents, by persisting. Her memories may be intact, helping to shield her from unsavory absences. I wonder if she thinks of herself as a memory in Zotikos' mind. If she were to linger in the air like a light breeze, her presence could not be denied. Zotikos will never tell me what it feels like not to have her around.

—I remember when I met the two of you at Café Central. Zotikos was so serious. Have you seen him lately?

—I saw him yesterday at Café Central.

—Was he serious?

—Yes, of course, he spoke about nothingness.

—Those are the books. He reads too many books, I think. When you see him next, tell him not to forget me.

She smells the cloves once more, and her entire face brightens. She must be remembering beautiful moments. That is a different kind of existence, an incorporeal one. Nevertheless, I am certain that whatever she is experiencing feels real to her. Her attachment to life is made of memories, and those seem to be strong and enduring.

—I'll tell Zotikos not to forget you. But if he does, would you be hurt by that?

—Perhaps, I don't know. I won't forget him; I don't

forget much. Everything is always there.

—No, there are times when we miss something.

—Perhaps, it so happens… sometimes.

Laura does not say goodbye. She simply turns around and walks into the thick of the market. In her mind, she is not leaving me behind; she is probably convinced her presence lingers in the air. Is she different from Carolina? They both tend to walk away, it seems. I do not know if Laura could ever be found again, not by me, by Zotikos. She may be content with no longer existing as a bodily presence for him. I also doubt that Zotikos would break out of his shell and pursue her. Carolina, on the other hand, wants to be found. On her terms, naturally. She expects me to look for her but does not allow me to find her. It is she who designs the encounters. They take place almost unexpectedly after I have given up on their probability. That may be why her absence is as substantial as a strong fragrance lingering in the air.

As I exit the market, I realize that I started the day looking for Laura. I needed confirmation, and I found one. There is no saltpeter in the air; it is absent. I should look no further for what is no longer there. But I could look for Carolina, not in the usual places, like the bridge or the old fountain, but where she is not expected to be found. The village is full of nonsignificant places where nobody is supposed to find anybody else. Unperceived by most, in control of my own insignificance, I can glide through the streets and perhaps discover Carolina in that presence of hers that exists outside of mine. Would she be surprised, or has she already prepared for such an unexpected encounter? I cannot tell.

Since I have no answers, nor an indication of what could happen, I start meandering the ordinary streets. Everyone looks like everyone else, and I look no different from them. I become part of the fabric of the village; I basically disappear. Could it be that Carolina is part of the fabric herself, that she becomes that self I need so much only when we are both present? Maybe she has never been absent, and she just ceases to exist outside of our ambit. She may begin to exist the moment she finds me, even if I have yet to lay my eyes on her.

I am careful not to rush my steps. I walk at a slow pace and pay attention to the mundane, that ubiquitous existence supporting my life. I do not want to miss anything or anybody. If she is present in this ordinary world, I want the opportunity to find her. So, I take to the shadows of an alley, turn the corner of a dirty street, and weave myself among other people who walk aimlessly. I look at their faces, and I recognize the humanity that inhabits this village. They seem to carry on unscathed by the absences that burden me. Maybe we all miss different things. Perhaps the absences are only personal.

A few meters in front of me, a woman walks, the likes of whom make me tremble. I follow her discreetly as she leaves a different imprint on this prosaic street. This is her, Carolina, in her world without me. This is her when she is absent. I get close to her, closer. This time it is me who places my hand on her shoulder. Startled, she turns around, but the face I encounter is unknown to me.

#

I consider the possibility of going elsewhere, traveling to another shore in search of the confirmation that escapes me. If the body of water has receded, if it simply ebbed beyond the curvature of the earth, it must be flowing abundantly on a foreign shore. This would be the case if what occurred was a displacement. Such a displacement would not negate the absence that I now experience, but it would give it a sense of abandonment, absence by abandonment, not by disappearance. That kind of absence will be more painful because it implies a rejection, the willful act of leaving someone behind. A disappearance, on the other hand, is an absence of non-existence. It does not imply abandonment or rejection; it is innocent and has no will.

If I were to clarify the nature of the absence, I would have to accept the potential emotional implications. There is a profound danger in that proposition. Perhaps an absence needs to be experienced and not understood, like when enjoying champagne without delving into chemistry or letting go of awareness while falling asleep. Sometimes we just do not know; sometimes, we are innocent.

I could also invent an explanation for what happened, contrive a history, give it a face and a name, and bring it into existence. That is what people call fiction, which may not differ much from the workings of our memory. Yes, I could allow for time to take its course, and upon later reflection, explain what may have happened in a way that satisfies my needs. The problem resides in enduring the passage of time under the significant emotional weight of an absence. That is yet another misfortune.

A photograph, taken at a particular place and time, does not lie. The image existed as such then, my memory may recreate the event and explain it in different ways, but the image is the image. Intrigued, I search for my collection of old photographs expecting some degree of confirmation. There are not many of them, only a handful. As I randomly look at them, I see my face expressing all sorts of emotions. It seems that at times I have been happy, but not often. I also see Carolina's face, happy more often. What I cannot find are photographs where we appear together, whether happy or otherwise. The image of one requires the active presence of the other as a photographer, as an observer. But nobody has acted as an observer for the two of us. I find no validation of our joint existence in the same place and time. What is absent is the image. This is not an absence by abandonment; this is an absence by neglect.

If I were to continue searching around for images,

objects, memories, or explanations, I would certainly confront many more absences. More is missing than what is found. And the longer one's life is the more opportunities for missing something. What matters, then, is not the number of absences but their emotional weight.

I better abandon this search, for it will bring nothing other than frustration. I should take my chances under the open sky where lives intersect each other, and memories are created. Alone, inside this apartment, I can debate the nature of everything I miss—I can build castles in my mind. Out in the open world, those castles need to bear the brunt of reality. A reality I may or may not be able to confirm. So, before I step out into the real world, I go to my library to reach for a book. Standing in front of the bookshelf, I close my eyes. I then reach out with my hand and grab a book at random. Once secure in my hand, I take care not to look at the title. The weight of the book tells me very little, just that it is not Joyce's *Ulysses*. And content with not knowing what story I carry with me; I leave my apartment in haste.

The streets seem to accept me. At least they offer no

resistance to my slow march. What matters now is not to allow my need for confirmation to direct my steps or my words. I should be able to forget all the absences and only deal with what is in front of me. Even if what I take as real is only a mirage, I will accept it as it is. What should be missing now is the sensation that something is missing.

Not paying much attention to the direction of my march, I meander through the village like a drifter. Although I know most of the streets very well, I try to focus on the odd angles and dark corners that abound. So, I walk through what is known but center my attention on the unknown. And as such, I march until finding myself in front of the municipal library with its impressive entrance, one I have breached only two or three times, for I prefer reading in solitude. There are many unknowns inside this building: thousands of authors I have never read and countless words I have never used. I pause for a moment, then I take a deep breath and venture through the entrance with my unveiled book in hand.

The reading room is half-empty and completely silent. I quietly walk to a table away from most people and take a seat. Many people are reading, some are sleeping, and nobody seems to care about me. I consider opening the book I brought along and start reading, but I hold myself back. Once I start reading, I will immediately recognize the book I grabbed at random from the bookshelf. Then the unknown would cease to exist. That would happen too soon and against my wishes for the day. I would like for the unknown to last longer, to displace any confirmatory possibility.

I look around from where I am sitting and see the sign for the fiction section. That is where the real stories gather, waiting for a reader to bring them alive. The potential is immense; the entire universe of human feelings, thought processes, lies, fears, and hope is accumulated between the covers of those books. Reading is not about discovery, for the human condition has been dissected many times over since the age of Homer. Reading is about feeling, an emotional journey initiated by the writer and later consummated by the reader. The book, thus, encapsulates the writer's soul in a state of suspended absence that becomes a presence only in the act of reading.

I get up from the table and make my way to the fiction section with my book in hand. The books on the tall shelves are catalogued in that special order that only librarians understand. But I am not looking for any special book now. Nor am I interested in reading the titles. I just want to feel the accumulation of the souls of so many writers. Each closed book represents a fraction of the human condition, of who we are as people. Each writer emphasizes a certain kind of feeling over others. But, cumulatively, they reveal the universe at large.

I palpate the book I brought with me to get an estimate of its width—about two centimeters. Like a Braille reader, I then run my fingers through the books on the shelves until coming across a book of similar width. But that is only half of the equation. Then, without looking at the title, I compare the height of both books and realize they are different; the book that I brought is taller. So, I repeat the blind exercise until my hand finds a book similar in width and height to the book I grabbed at random from my bookshelf at home. I then swap the books. One unknown replaces another; one writer occupies the soul of another. What I now have in my hands is a purer unknown, and that fills me with joy. I steal not; I borrow. The reverse process will take place once I unveil the absence this writer hid between the covers of this book. I will drink from this writer's emotions, and I will share them with Zotikos.

On the way out of the municipal library, I decide to alter my approach and start walking in a specific direction. I am not drifting now; I am heading toward Café Central. As I am gathering speed, the thought of Carolina crosses my mind, an uninvited thought this is. I cannot afford to think about her at this moment. If I were to imagine her presence, I would act as if I were looking for her. This could potentially arouse her desire to observe me, which may lead to an encounter if, indeed, that is the mechanism giving birth to our meetings. I doubt that is the way things happen. However, I need to be careful. The weight of aggregate unknowns can be crushing.

There are many routes leading to Café Central. None of them are totally straight, but some are more convoluted than others. What matters now is to arrive there and begin the writing process in the most direct way. Zotikos will present multiple convolutions; such is his nature. He will try to derail the effort because it is in derailing that he finds his way. His thought process is sinusoidal, and that allows him to approach the unknown without perturbing it. Although he has not openly agreed to collaborate with me in writing the book, he has no options but to do so. He is suffering from an absence that he is afraid to accept. I am confronting an absence that I cannot validate. The common element, that which is not there, will serve as the fulcrum of our effort.

This time, from a distance, I recognize Zotikos' silhouette sitting at our table. He seems to recognize my silhouette as well because he waves at me. The fact that he acknowledges my arrival from far away tells me he is anxious to express something, even if Zotikos denies such need, as he will likely do. I wave back at him from afar. He immediately looks down at the book he is reading and ignores the rest of the world around him. He will not look up again until after I am sitting at the table for about five minutes. This time he is the first one to speak.

—I've been sitting here for a while, and I've come to realize that I don't recognize myself.

—What about you has changed?

—Everything and nothing at the same time. It is like looking at a mannequin that resembles me, behaves like me, but it is clearly not me. You just saw me from a distance, did I look like myself?

—You did look like yourself, but I was surprised when you waved at me. That's not what you normally do.

—That's precisely the strangeness I'm referring to. I've done things that I've never expected to do, like waving at you or thinking about Laura while having a pastis.

—Maybe you're becoming more like yourself.

—I cannot become anything other than what I've already been. Whatever this is, it's foreign to me.

—Are you afraid of yourself?

—No, I'm afraid of what I don't know about myself.

—I need a pastis if we're going to talk about that.

By the time I think about signaling Maurice, he is already approaching our table with his tray. Nothing on his face reveals great surprise; we must look no different to him. We are sitting at the same table. Zotikos is reading a book; we talk to each other from time to time, never raise our voices, and never seem scared. Just like everything else, this too may change.

—If there are aspects about yourself that you don't know, then those aspects cannot alter the concept you already have of yourself because that concept is based only on what is known to you. So, there's nothing to fear.

—Once again, nothingness.

—Yes, nothingness… And what's the problem with that?

—I'm not used to it. I expect everything to be perpetually tangible and palpable. Don't talk to me about voids, vacuums, emptiness, or absences. They're not part of my life; they don't exist for me.

—So, how do you manage when something isn't there any longer?

—I turn to reading a book.

—Does that solve the problem?

—It used to solve the problem, but not anymore.

—No matter how many books you read, Laura is absent, and you're aware that she's absent.

—Yes, she's absent.

Zotikos closes his book and turns his eyes away from me. He must be staring into the unspecified space found between buildings, above the street, among the passers-by—that space containing nothing.

CHAPTER SIX

If I were to scrutinize my bookshelf, I would probably guess the title of the book I left at the library in replacement for the one I took from there. I would certainly recognize the two adjacent books, and my memory would provide the image of the absent one. So, I avoid looking at the bookshelf, like I avoid looking at the book's title in my hands. All I know is that they are roughly the same size, but what they talk about is unknown to me.

Better to start with an unknown. Sitting at my desk, in the solitude of my apartment, I open the unveiled book on a random page and read a single paragraph. It talks about the passage of time, about death, and about a minor incident that had been completely ignored. That is sufficient for me. I close the book and read no longer. I then put the book inside a drawer where the shadows hide its title. I have all I need to start writing my half of the book. Zotikos will write his own half in his very own solitude. Now that he has faced and accepted an absence, he has no choice but to write about it.

The passage I just read refers to an ignored incident.

It is impossible for me to guess the nature of that incident. But it was ignored, and that makes all the difference. Then there was mention of the passage of time. Time is of the essence. When I consider the absence of the blue above the sand, I realize that timing remains a mystery. Did that absence occur at a single point in time, or did it evolve gradually over days and weeks? This is a great unknown to me, which is precisely what I am striving for. However, if I am invested in writing about something unknown, at least I need to immerse myself in the emotional repercussions of that unknown. So, I ask myself if I have ignored the emotional aspects of the absence? What if I have not felt the absence in its entirety? That would create a new absence, one of emotions. This new absence would hinder the understanding of the original absence, which is unacceptable.

What did I really feel when I stood at the shore and faced a vast desert in front of me? Was it fear, sadness, or anxiety, perhaps? The first reaction was disbelief; I am certain of that. But disbelief is not a feeling; it is an intellectual refusal. It happens when I see something that counters my accepted reality and questions its existence. The relevant element is the emotion that follows the confirmation of a new perceived reality. I think I felt abandoned, forgotten. That magnificent blue, which I cherish so much, went elsewhere and left me behind. I do not know why it happened. I do not know if I could have prevented it. And the worst aspect is that I cannot confirm if the crib of all waves has disappeared from everyone's reality or only from mine.

Then there was the silence. Like a submerged cathedral, a silence like I've never experienced before. I did welcome that solemn and profound silence. It filled me with a sense of amplitude and lightness. Without the absence, however, I am almost certain the silence would not have occurred. And because they are intertwined, I will not be able to confirm the existence of the silence without confirming that of the absence. This makes me feel disenchanted, if not saddened.

Considering that I am confronting several unknowns, those feelings cannot be fully confirmed because they could be modified the moment things become clearer. At this juncture, all I have are questions and almost no answers. That is precisely the feeding ground for anxiety with that eviscerating feeling I refuse to experience. That is why I need to write this book, to gain some perspective and exorcise the budding anguish.

I place that thought process on hold, take the book out of the drawer, and open it again on some random page. This time the passage I read talks about the secret meaning of the world. It does not reveal the secret, it only refers to its existence. I would venerate the secret meaning of the world if it were to remain a secret. Only in being a secret would it retain its power and charm. The holder of the secret, on the other hand, would be immune to its fascination and not find it powerful nor charming. This forces me to admit that every unknown contains a certain allure. Certain unknowns may need to remain obscure. The world needs to have secrets. The question then arises, which are the unknowns that require clarification, and which should be ignored? Incidents have been ignored in this book, as I already read. Are those the secrets the world is keeping from us? Is the passage of time, with its power and charm, the maker of all secrets?

The world outside my apartment contains a legion of unknowns. Perhaps the one that affects me more intimately is the whereabouts of Carolina when she is not with me. The truth is that I have never attempted to elucidate that information. I have accepted each of her departures as I accept the natural order of things. I have never questioned them. Where she is this very moment, I do not know. Since it is natural for her to leave after one of our rendezvous, I have refrained from wanting to know more. I cannot say that she withholds that information from me because I have not asked her directly. In this case, I should not consider her whereabouts a secret, in the sense of information being withheld purposefully from me, but as an unknown. I have lived with that unknown because out of its darkness the encounters materialize.

Likewise, I cannot comprehend why the desert extends from the shore far into the horizon. It is clearly not the natural order of things. On the contrary, it is an aberration. This unknown hurts me because nothing seems to materialize out of its darkness. This unknown deserves to be unraveled, elucidated. But how? I have not been able to confirm its existence. I do not know if it is indeed an unknown.

I decide to return to the pages of the book in search of answers. If the outside world is not shedding any light on the unknown, maybe this book can. Perhaps there is a central light in this book, one that does not burn me. The exercise of fanning the pages promises randomness, and my hand stops once again on an improbable passage. This one speaks about a meeting in the afternoon when what is being written will be shared. It also speaks about secrets being thrown into the crib of all waves. A suggestion, perhaps an indication, or maybe mere coincidence. Could it be that in its disappearance, the blue above the sand sequestered all secrets? Could it be that the absence I feel is an absence of secrets and the silence an absence of whispers? I must close this book now, for I could be burnt.

I am not afraid of failing. Let failing assimilate me. What frightens me is not knowing that I have failed. I wonder if my reticence to revisiting the shore is a failure on my part. Should I not stand in front of the former divide and scrutinize the horizon? Should I not look for traces of the former body of water? Should I not confront other people and have them look at the horizon and then look into their eyes for answers. Only the fear of confirmation prevents me from doing any of that. And that fear is a clear failure. But, if I know that

I have failed, then there would be nothing to fear. The problem is that I am not sure if I have failed or not.

Further ruminations will only bring doom and paralysis. My thoughts will need to remain suspended in the air, weightless, like soap bubbles. The book will need to rest on the table and accept its anonymity. I need to render myself outside of these walls and grapple with any unknown or absence that reality wants to bestow on me. It is not possible to write about an entity that escapes me. How could I commune with Zotikos if I cannot touch that which I fear?

I return to the streets, to the alleys, to the flow of people that seem unconcerned. The clouds look down on me, unconcerned as well, and so are the dogs and their masters. I must be alone on this quest because the air shows no haste, and the birds keep their flapping rhythm. It does not matter in which direction I look; everything appears to be just as it has always been. There are no wrinkles auguring the passage of time. It all looks natural.

I allow my feet to control their own stepping. I impose no direction. Let reality dictate my whereabouts and my most immediate future. But in so doing, I notice that with every step I walk further and further from the shore, as if I were intent on avoiding it. But I am not intent on anything other than facing the absences. And since I let my thoughts suspended in the air, this must be my unconscious mind trying to protect me. So, I assert control of my steps and redirect my walk toward the shore. That is where failure may be waiting for me.

As I get closer to the shore, my pulse begins to accelerate, and I find it difficult to breathe. I stop for a moment and close my eyes. I try to think of nothing; I try to forge a dark curtain in front of me. But the light traverses my eyelids, and I see a redness instead. These must be the sun rays bouncing off the extended body of water, or perhaps red blood rushing to my head. I cannot be stopped now. I take a deep breath and head directly toward the shore, toward the openness.

There are moments in a person's life when sand turns to stone, when the drops of doubt coalesce to form an uncomfortable puddle of certitude. This is what I feel when in front of me; there is nothing but what I feared. The unmentionable has departed. It is no longer. It is absent. The dry seabed extends widely, revealing the previously submerged ravines, the seaweed now dry. I close my eyes once more to reject what is evident. But when I open them again, the absence is utterly present in all its weight and might. Not only has the mirror of the moon vanished, but so are the witnesses to the occurrence, for I am one among no one else.

I forget about time and its subjugating force. I forget about past, present, and future books. I forget about Carolina and our improbable meetings. I forget about all my failures. What matters now is to hollow out my mind, discard all ballast, and create room for this monumental absence. The certitude of this absence pulverizes any doubts, and my life now includes this certitude.

Alone as I am, facing the prospect of a different reality, I yield to the strangeness of the moment. The universe must have a reason for acting this way, but it does not share it with me. Perhaps because the universe operates in a much larger context, much larger than the insignificant life I live. This could be a personal absence only or one that touches the village and the world that surrounds the village. I cannot tell—but I can write about it.

CHAPTER SEVEN

I am the first one to arrive. The table seems a little surprised to see me at this early hour, but it does not react. It stays firmly planted on its four legs and offers its horizontal back to support my glass of pastis, my book, my desires. The table does not know that I am alone. However, it must sense the absence of Zotikos, of the energy he imparts to our discussions. Without Zotikos, Café Central is not the same. Like an empty train station, it dies a little.

The promise of the morning is rather simple: the day will follow. Infallible that promise. My waiting for Zotikos is more complex than that, for it promises nothing concrete. What will ensue is variable, movable, even porous. But his arrival is imminent and inevitable because Zotikos cannot be himself elsewhere. He pretends not to need to come here, to this table, to face me and ignore me. But he knows that I know he yearns to come here. And so do I.

As this day proceeds, I will attempt to align my mind with that of Zotikos. Not because of weakness on my part. I have the courage to tackle any absence on my own. But because the absence he tries to ignore, that of Laura, is of humankind. On the other hand, my absence of the mirror of the moon is impersonal yet universal. And then there is the myriad of other absences. Like when Carolina vanishes, when a vast silence replaces all earthly sounds, or when the sun buries itself under the redness. They all matter; they all bleed. It may be in the reconciliation of them all that I could finally understand the curvature of an absence.

He arrives, Zotikos. As he walks rather slowly toward the table, I notice his regard and get a sense that he is dejected, or perhaps tired. Under his arm, he brings a book, of course. But his eyes are not as bright as they usually are. Once he sits down at our table, he takes a long look at my face, at my eyes, as if he were looking for a place to hide. He comes from having bled; I sense it.

—I've been waiting for you for a while.

—Your wait is over. Now you can go on with the rest of your day.

—This is where the day is at.

—If you say so. But I'm not convinced.

—Yes, everything is here. What we know and what

we don't know. It's all here.

—You're here. I can see that. You even came earlier than me. Now, I'm here as well. But when I reach out with my hand, I touch nothing.

—You're touching that book, and that book is touching someone else.

—If you say so. But I'm still not convinced. As a matter of fact, I'm convinced about nothing.

—That's a perfect conviction for this day. Out of nothingness, we emerge.

He becomes silent and sits at the table. He opens his book and begins to read. For the moment, he is lost in a world that is not his world. He has abandoned the uneasy reality, the hard nothingness. His mind will fluctuate between the fictional world and the one here at the table. I will be ignored and resurrected multiple times, yet our minds will engage with each other during the day.

I consider where to start. The first order of events is to make sure Zotikos gets a glass of pastis. I raise my arm to signal Maurice, but I do not see him anywhere. After a minute or two, I stand and look around the Café. Maurice is nowhere to be found. This is not normal. I go to the back of the Café where the cook tells me he has not seen Maurice today, that he is missing. He says not to worry that he will bring some pastis to our table.

I realize that Maurice is absent. Why is he absent today? Will he be absent tomorrow? Why is he absent, to begin with? I expect him to be here as he always is. That is the natural order of things. However, if I had not expected him to be here, I would not be experiencing his absence. Habits breed expectations, and expectations may not be fulfilled. I must beware of expectations, for they may usher a legion of absences into my life.

At the table, Zotikos has closed his book and seems distracted with his thoughts. When I join him, he ignores my presence and remains silent. Something is boiling inside of him. A caravan of thoughts is marching through his mind. What he is considering could be derived from the fictional world he is reading about or from his wounds. I am not sure, so I decide to address reality.

—Maurice is absent.

—So is Laura.

—And many more people and multiple things. But we remain.

—For the moment.

—Yes, for the moment, we remain. So, we better relish this moment.

—I was relishing my reading until the thought of Laura interrupted the flow. It came from nowhere. It just landed in my consciousness unannounced.

—Are you surprised?

—I'm surprised about the vulnerability of my mind. Shouldn't I be able to fend away that kind of intrusion? It's like a violation, an infringement.

—Thoughts come and go. Like the waves in the... Like the waves.

The cook brings two glasses with ice, a bottle of pastis, and some water. He leaves it all on the table and tells us to serve ourselves, for he is no waiter. Zotikos prepares his glass and returns to the silence of his reading. He acknowledges being vulnerable, and that must frighten him tremendously—he who hides behind a well-defended wall of stones.

I catch a glimpse of the book he is reading and manage to identify the title, *Nausea*. He will find a fellow traveler in Sartre. Yes, the concept of nothingness is corrupting him. He can touch it with his hands. I get the impression that he is terrified by the unmeasurable vastness of such nothingness. Like a boy who stands at the shore, regarding the crib of all waves for the first time; this is a brutal confrontation with the meagerness of our human nature.

When he reads, Zotikos maintains a completely neutral facial expression. He seems to process all emotions behind that wall of stones. The cracks on the wall become visible only when he questions something. And once he realizes his exposure, he quickly hides behind the wall of stones again. He does not smile much, and I have never heard him sing. I know very little about Zotikos, like he knows very little about me. We come to this table to share our mutual absence of knowledge of each other. However, we are similar—we are both missing something.

A strange and heavy air flows into Café Central, making me worry about the kind of day that will follow. It will either be a very long day or a short and dense one. Already from the start, Maurice has gone missing, and Zotikos is behind his wall of stones. I could thwart further misfortunes by running back to my apartment and closing all windows. But I came here in the early morning with the clear intention to align my mind with that of Zotikos, to reconcile our losses. So, once again, I interrupt Zotikos in his reading.

—Why do you read that book?

—Because I haven't read it before.

—What do you expect to find in its pages?

—Nothing.

—You don't have to read that book to find nothing; nothing is around you already.

—I've come to realize that. The book is only a confirmation.

—Does your nothingness have a color?

—Yes, it's purple. I don't know if you have the same experience, but I touch a purplish vacuum when I reach out with my hands.

—I don't have that experience. I simply look out and don't see things as they used to be.

—What's missing?

—The blue above the sand is missing.

—If you don't see a certain blue, and if nothing is what occupies its space, then it would have attained a purple color. If you don't see that purplish vacuum, then nothing *is* missing. That is, nothingness is not actually there.

—I want to believe you, but I don't.

—You don't have to believe me, like I don't have to read Sartre, like we don't have to sit at this table and drink pastis, like we won't write that book you spoke about.

—We are already writing that book. We are turning its pages as we speak.

—A purple book that will be.

He refers to purple as a representation of what is not there. Perhaps because of its rarity in nature. Purple conjures magic, mystery, dignity, royalty. But above all, purple is the color of mourning. The loss of Laura must be hurting him deeply, even if he fails to admit it as such. I do not feel the same way. I am not mourning the vanished mirror of the moon, for I do not love it as a person loves another person. The fear of additional absences is what ravages me. Once a great body of water goes missing, what could be next? The earth below my feet, the sky itself, or the air I breathe?

I know what Zotikos has lost and the resulting absence, but he ignores the nature of the absence I am confronting. If I were to explain it to him in simple and direct words, he would probably dismiss it as a great lunacy of mine. He would likely revert to his reading and ignore me for the rest of the day. For him to understand the devastating consequences of a vanishing blue, he would have to experience it in his own flesh. He would need to stand at the shore and look with his very eyes at the emptiness in front of him. Only then would he be on the same emotional turmoil as I am. Likewise, for me to feel a similar loss, my encounters with Carolina would need to come to an end. But I have no control over those happenstances. Furthermore, I ignore when the next encounter takes place. So, it is possible that they may have already come to an end without me knowing—an additional absence that will be.

The day wants to forge ahead irrespective of whether Zotikos and I align our minds or not. In fact, the day owes nothing to us, and it will not delay its progress. Zotikos is content with reading and licking his wounds, only slightly. I could try to forget that the world, as I once knew it, has changed. I could simply watch the world spin and let myself get caught in its whirling winds. But that is not why I came to this table in the early morning. I need to elucidate what is missing. That need hangs over my awareness, and it will not cease to exist. I have no other choice. Thus, I sample some of the pastis and interrupt Zotikos once again.

—There comes a time when what you don't know can hurt you.

—What I don't know doesn't exist for me.

—You're absolutely wrong. It does exist. And if you ignore it, you're bound to get hurt.

—How could I even grasp that which I don't know?

—You must go in search of it.

—But how could I lead my search if I don't know what I'm searching for?

—That's the predicament. You may need to search for nothing. You may need to touch that purple vacuum you abhor.

—There's nothing there.

—On the contrary, there's plenty, although some of it is missing.

—Then, bring me to that nothingness.

#

The road to the shore is paved with unknowns. The

first one is Zotikos himself. I have never seen him outside of Café Central. I do not know how he behaves away from that table we share. Does he see the outside world as I see it? Will he follow me to the shore, or will he become mute, turn around, and disappear? Would he experience the same absence as I do and hear the same silence? Then there is the path itself. Even though I know in which direction to walk, what if I lose my way? Would the shore still be there, or did it abandon the village and went in search for the crib of all waves? And even if we arrive at the shore together, what would be waiting there for us? Perhaps these are purple questions… I do not know.

Zotikos walks alongside me in complete silence. He does not ask where we are going. He seems to accept that we are walking toward a place where nothing is to be found. Maybe it matters little to him that there may be nothing, or perhaps he is silent because there is a great turmoil in his mind. His steps are relatively light, giving me the impression that he has disentangled his mind from his body.

As we turn a corner and take a street leading to the market, I see the silhouette of a woman in the distance that gives me pause. I slow my pace and confirm that it is Laura walking in our direction. Yes, it is Laura. Coincidence, perhaps, or just the natural order of things. Next to me, Zotikos maintains his silence and his countenance ignoring the angst of the moment. Since I am not the arbiter of the world, nor a teller of fortunes, I continue walking toward the inevitable.

Just as we are about to cross each other on the sidewalk, we come to a full stop. In front of me is Laura, next to me is Zotikos, and not too far is the shore and the great absence. Laura seems content and not surprised by the encounter. The bouquet of white flowers she carries in her hands oozes a deeply satisfying scent that turns all around us. She then offers an ample smile and says, "Everything is always there." And with those words she continues her march away from us and does not look back. I expect that Zotikos will break his silence after this fortuitous encounter. And he does.

—That was a beautiful fragrance. Intense and disquieting.

—The fragrance was disquieting…

—Yes, it went deep inside of me like an underground river. I can still feel the reverberations. Where did it come from? How did that scent find us?

—That scent did not arrive on its own; it came accompanied.

—A scent needs no company; it just floats in the air, invisible but tangible.

—Those were white flowers you smelled.

—Maybe the fragrance of white flowers, but where are the flowers?

—They were here just a minute ago, right in front of you.

—There was nothing in front of me other than a fragrance; where has it gone?

—Zotikos, that fragrance is an absence.

The world around us is impersonal, but we see the world in a personal way. Zotikos may not see the world in the same way I see it. Or, perhaps, he does not allow himself to see all that the world proposes. Laura is missing in his life, and that reality may have grown roots. Maybe the emotional space that Laura occupied is no longer available to him. Maybe her absence has infiltrated all his sensorial capacities. One cannot see what is not there.

We continue our march. This time Zotikos walks

ahead of me, and I simply follow him. He does not seem to be interested in following any direction. He turns right or left in an apparently random fashion. He may be trying to find that fragrance again, or to the contrary, he may be walking away from it. I cannot tell, for he has gone back to his silence, and his face reveals no emotion.

The streets exist to take our steps. They lie on their backs, immovable, accepting. They do not show us the way either. And when our thoughts bounce against the walls that line them up, they do not try to decipher them. They conduct without conducting; they do not applaud our steps. They create no maze, for the maze is only in our minds. We course through them; we flow, we are the ones in motion. The streets cannot tell north from south, a beginning from an end. We are the ones making such attributions. And if we were to turn a corner and leave a street behind, the street would not be offended.

The seemingly random walk initiated by Zotikos takes us closer and closer to the shore. Even though we are moving in a tortuous way, it is now evident that we will soon get there. He may be moving in the direction of the shore by conscious design or by a feeling of camaraderie. I cannot tell. I simply refrain from making any comments and embrace the forthcoming encounter with what is missing. Does it matter how we approach an absence, from what angle, at what speed, with our eyes closed or open? Perhaps not.

With every one of our steps, the world becomes quiet and quieter. And when we enter the realm of an exquisite silence, I know we have arrived at the shore. I hesitate; I feel uncertain about extending my regard far into the horizon to grapple with what I fear, that the caravels have not returned. But I need to elucidate what is missing, so I do look, I confront, and I am dismayed at the vastness of the absence. What is not there continues not to be there.

Next to me, Zotikos appears to be at ease. While he contemplates the openness in front of him, the angles of his face soften. He even offers a faint smile. He seems to be in profound communion with the moment. But not a word comes out of his lips. And in so doing, he deepens the silence. A shared silence that does not reveal the disparity of our emotions. I really need his words now.

—Zotikos, can you see the caravels?

—No, they've been gone for centuries.

—And why haven't they returned?

—Because people forgot about them. The moment we forget about something it ceases to exist. Then, if we happen to remember, it may be too late already. That's why we need a collective memory to guarantee a minimum of continuous existence.

—Does Laura exist for you?

—When I remember her, she does. But there are times when I forget her completely.

—Do you miss her?

—Only when I remember her.

—And what makes you remember her?

—I don't know what triggers those memories. There's a randomness to them. Sometimes, when I try to hold on to one of those memories, I end up empty-handed. I hold nothing.

—Isn't that what you're looking for, nothing?

—You're once again proposing misfortunes. There's no reason to think of nothingness right now.

—Well, I do remember the caravels. They were here, right in front of us.

—But they don't exist anymore, they are history.

—They were here, Zotikos.

—They are now missing.

—Yes, they are.

Clearly, Zotikos does not see the world as I do. I do not see the world as he does. We see what the other one is missing, but we cannot see what we are missing ourselves. It is in the not seeing that an absence is created. Then memory plays a role with its intermittent and taunting ways. If we were courageous enough to forget, many absences would be eliminated, and more clarity could be enjoyed. But once an absence begins to curve in front of us, we lose our sight and our freedom.

Nothing moves around us, not even the air. The sun makes no gestures, and the seagulls are silent. A peaceful veil has descended upon us, separating this moment from the rest of the day. Zotikos is not alarmed; his face reveals no surprises, no bewilderment. In front of him, the world must be intact. The shore must contain all the elements necessary to be a shore. He is clearly not impacted by any absence in this very instant.

On the other hand, when I regard the horizon, the same absence comes to greet me. As immense as it was before, as intimidating. Its nature remains unchanged. And I know this is not an illusion because the feeling of emptiness is real; I can taste a certain acidity in my mouth.

With nothing to float on, the caravels are certain never to return. Not even the most intact memory could make the caravels drag themselves through the desert sands. It is time for me to turn my back on that image. So, as the day resumes its course, I decide to join it. I take Zotikos by the elbow and lead the march away from the shore. We walk together, but we do not talk to each other, perhaps because each of us senses a certain uneasiness inside of the other, to each his turmoil. Perhaps by walking together, we validate each other's absence.

Walking can only take place in one direction, toward Café Central. I do not know where Zotikos lives, neither does he know where I live. That is inconsequent. We share our table, our minds, and the pleasure of drinking pastis. We now share the experience of missing something. We also share a certain clairvoyance about what each other is missing. What else is there to share? Perhaps a path toward a deeper understanding, or maybe the writing of a book.

Once we arrive at Café Central and occupy our table, Maurice shows up immediately with pastis, water, and ice. I am ecstatic to see him. He was not here before, but now he is. He is no longer missing. His absence was only temporary; it has been remedied. To what should I attribute this fortune? I could ask him what exactly happened. But if I did, I would probably get an answer. What would I do with that answer? I simply say to Maurice that I am happy to see him, to which he nods in response before he goes to take care of another table. I then turn to Zotikos, raise my glass, and make a toast.

—To the world as we know it!

—To what we don't know about the world!

—To the deepest silence!

—What silence is that?

—The one at the shore.

—At the shore, there was the sound of the surf and the incessant talk of the seagulls.

—To the return of the caravels!

—To the return of Laura!

Chapter Eight

It has been seven days and thirteen hours. I am starting to feel tired now. Perhaps I should have rested on the seventh day as the wise god did, or so they say. But I am not that wise, and I am far from being a god, not even a lesser one. Besides, I am not creating a universe; I am only creating half of a book of fiction. Clearly, to that vast universe, the book amounts to nothing. Likewise, I am nothing to that same universe; however, I am the universe to my own self. And in this personal universe of mine, the book matters. The book shares my breath, knows about my dreams, and handles my fears with care. Like a good companion, the book waits for me at my desk until I am ready to talk. Then, it listens.

But I am tired now. Seven days and thirteen hours inside of my apartment is a long time. My hands now feel like lead. I abandon the writing and step back from the empty page. All those hours inside the apartment, away from Café Central, without re-visiting the shore… Those hours weigh me down. When I take a closer look at the text, I realize I have written a great amount. I notice that behind some of the paragraphs, an absence seems to glow. It emits a radiant but dark light. I have written those paragraphs, but I do not know what is buried under them. I accept that unknown.

I refrain from reading what I have written so far. I am afraid that if I were to read any of it, the underlying currents bringing me closer to the absence would be disrupted. I need a reader who would stand no such risk. I need Zotikos. His reading, then, could be more central to the text's intellectual life than my writing, and consequently, he could be more important to a text than I am. In the same way, Zotikos needs me to be his reader. If he is to open about his losses, he needs someone who would listen, as a good book would.

Seven days and thirteen hours. Zotikos may feel abandoned by me. He may interpret my absence from Café Central as a rejection. After such a long time of recurrent seances at the same table, of endless conversations, of raising multiple glasses of pastis, after all of that, then, nothing. But Zotikos has an oblique way of considering life. He may accept such nothingness as a present from me. He says he wants to touch nothing, and nothing is what I have offered him this last week. It is entirely possible that he is at Café Central this very moment, drinking pastis and taking advantage of my absence to write his part of the book. Or, maybe he has gone to the shore to listen to the surf and the incessant talking of the seagulls. I never know with Zotikos.

It is time to move away from my desk. It is time to consider the outside world once again. I step up to my window and confirm that nothing has changed, only the shadows. Everything seems to be as it was. The accumulation of words cannot change the world, but it can change the mind. Maybe the shadows inside my mind have changed. They could be longer, or rounder, or taken a bluish tone. But this is not the time to look inside my mind. This is the time to burst out into the world.

I assemble the unfinished manuscript, unbound pages with a little number at the bottom. Not all the pages will survive at the end; I am aware of that. Some will be discarded; others will be expanded upon, while others may be forgotten. Regardless of its uncertain future, I put the manuscript inside my portfolio and my two feet out on the street. Without delay, I head for Café Central in search of my reader, Zotikos.

As I reflect on Zotikos' possible reactions after reading my part of the manuscript, I need to consider the most basic of them, that he will have no reaction at all. It is entirely possible for him to read my contribution to the book and not say a word about it. If that were the case, the manuscript would only exist for him since he is the one bringing it into existence. For me, it would remain an unfinished project. In the same vein, if he shows me what he is writing and I offer no comments, he would be equally deprived of completion. We are mutually interdependent; we are each other's complementary authors. There is an implicit parallelism between my text, his reading, his text, and my reading.

It occurs to me that Zotikos is capable of not writing anything whatsoever. I know he is constantly reading, but I have never seen him in the process of writing. Yes, I have read his book of poems where he plays with words, or the words play with him—an imagistic book about what is right in front of him, or about what objects and emotions can become. I have not read anything by him on what is not there, on that nothingness he wants to touch so desperately. What words would he use if he touches nothingness and then attempts to write about that experience? Would he simply produce blank pages?

Soon enough, my steps bring me to the bridge leading into the old part of the village. I slow down and think about Carolina and the multiple encounters that have taken place here. Maybe she has come to this bridge in search of me during the last seven days. If she did, she did not find me. Has she missed me? After how many times of coming to the bridge and not finding me would she stop coming altogether? She is not here now. Or, at least, I do not see her. I better cross this bridge before another misfortune attacks me.

From a distance, Café Central looks like any other establishment of its kind. An outdoor terrace with a few tables, several potted plants that do not want to be there, an interior salon dimly lit, walls covered with posters announcing products no longer sold anywhere, a mirror above the bar, patrons, and waiter Maurice, of course. Everything occupies its rightful place. The only component missing is Zotikos, who is not sitting at our table at this moment. Unperturbed, I take my customary place and signal Maurice. As soon as he arrives with the bottle of pastis, he asks me where I have been. I tell him I have spent the last few days in my apartment. He asks if I have been sick. I tell Maurice that I feel very well. I tell him I was writing and writing; he smiles and walks away.

What is customary is healthy. Or so thinks Maurice. A change in routine could only stem from adversity. My absence, then, could not have been voluntary; some tragedy, illness, or calamity must have caused it. It is clearly ominous to him when the natural order of things falls into disarray. But Maurice is not alone; I am his accomplice. Why is the absence at the shore so devastating to me? Because I have become accustomed to seeing the color blue above the sand? Because a different order, like an extended desert at the shore, is not part of my history? Because I have yet to form memories of that new order?

While I formulate those questions, time advances, and Zotikos' absence begins to sediment. I would have expected for him to arrive already, with a book under his arm and his distracted look. But he has not arrived, and I have no way to explain why. I could do as Maurice and suspect that he is ill. I could also refuse to count on what is customary and expect nothing at all. Maybe Zotikos wants me to stretch my arm and touch nothing as he does. Or maybe Zotikos does not expect me to come to our table any longer. He could have restructured his own order. There are no answers to those questions. So, I resolve to drink some pastis and wait for nothing.

I open the portfolio and pull out the manuscript. What have I written? What is the real meaning of the text? I abstain from reading the first sentence, for it may be misleading. Neither would I read the last sentence, for it may not be the final one. Tempted as I am to find a certain sense of last week's efforts, I open the manuscript at a random page. I know I am taking a risk. But after a sip of pastis, I dare to read an entire paragraph. I close the manuscript as soon as I finish reading, and put it back inside the portfolio. The words I read begin to swirl inside my mind. They align themselves in multiple ways and assume various meanings. But the text eludes my deciphering. My reading has derailed their intended meaning. Those words need to be read by a mind other than mine. They need to be read by Zotikos, he who is absent.

The world spins on its own axis without a will. The universe expands or contracts without willing to do so. I amount to very little in comparison. So, why should my wish for Zotikos' presence be of importance? I cannot *will* him to be here. I do not have such power. The one thing I could effectively do at this moment is wait. Only after the passage of time will Zotikos' absence be confirmed. Only then. But how much time needs to elapse? This afternoon, the entire day? Do I have to come to Café Central on numerous occasions and sit at this table alone to conclude that Zotikos is resolutely absent? I cannot answer those questions.

As I allow for the flow of time to slip through, I come to realize that there is a certain magic in waiting. He who waits has an expectation, the expectation that a desired change is inevitable. That perceived inevitability could give birth to hope if the event is a cherished one. How about the expectation for the ignoble? In that case, the expectation could give birth to fear. Perhaps I hope for Zotikos to return and fear that he may not do so. But for any of those emotions to become manifest, time needs to be in the process of flowing, and confirmations need to be pending. That is the magic in waiting.

Somehow, I also expect that Zotikos will be interested in reading my manuscript. The fact that I need him to read it does not imply that he has a desire to do so. Furthermore, even if he reads the manuscript, being oblique as he is, he could very easily keep his impressions to himself and never share them with me. In that case, my part of the book would have been completed since he would have given life to the literary meaning of the text, but I would ignore the face of my creation. Granted, every book has as many faces as there are readers. But the face that Zotikos will impart to the manuscript is important for me. Because, like me, he is amid an absence.

Time has not stopped. I know because the shadows assume a different angle, and my glass of pastis is empty. What matters is not for how long I have been waiting. But, that in the process, I have forgotten about the caravels, the mirror of the moon, or the impossibility at the shore. Maybe our minds can only handle one absence at a time. Maybe it is inhuman to harbor an emptiness larger than ourselves. I clearly reject such misfortune. So, I grab my portfolio and walk away from Café Central, hoping and fearing at the same time.

#

The bridge knows not to move; it is waiting for me. It invites me to walk on its back. It wants to hold my weight, to suspend me in the air. Why would I refuse? It is on this bridge, while detached from solid ground, that many meetings have taken place. Instead of crossing the bridge, I advance to the middle of it and stop walking. Exposed, suspended, I hope for an encounter with Carolina.

Between one side and another, between the hope of seeing her and the disillusion of missing her, between the morning and the evening, right in the middle of nothing, I stand waiting. Is it me who decides to come to this bridge, or are the forces of habit the ones that push me to stand here? I cannot tell. If I were to keep on walking, it is very likely that I will not see Carolina. If I were to remain here and wait for the universe to behave in the way it has in the past, I might have a chance to see Carolina. So, maybe what coerces me to stand here and wait are the forces of expectation. But, expectation is a capricious creature. I expected to meet with Zotikos at Café Central, and he did not materialize. I expected to hear the incoming surf at the shore,

144

and I was immersed in silence instead. He who expects may not be gratified.

Carolina then places her hand on my shoulder. A simple gesture that confirms her presence and surprises me, for I was not expecting her to appear this way. She does not greet me; she behaves nonchalantly, as if she had been next to me for the past seven days. She contemplates the singing waters of the river as they flow completely unencumbered and does not say a word. This is not like the silence at the shore, but a silence it is. So, I decide to break it.

—You surprised me. I didn't see you coming.

—Oh! I heard your steps on the bridge and came to greet you.

—Why haven't you said a word yet?

—The river speaks for me.

—I do hear the river singing.

—So, then you hear me.

—What are you singing about?

—A simple song about nothing.

—Everything seems to be about nothing.

—That may be true, but it doesn't matter. Tell me, what's in your portfolio?

The portfolio enters the realm of expectations. It has been very light up until this moment, but now it weighs like lead and pulls down on my arm. I consider taking out the manuscript and letting Carolina read some of it. No, no. I refrain. I have yet to read it myself, and Zotikos has not read it either. Furthermore, I am not completely sure what it is about. Why set the unknowns on fire?

—There's a manuscript in my portfolio, but I don't really know what I wrote about.

—Perfect, like I don't know what my song is about.

—Yes, we understand each other.

—Do you really think we understand each other? I'm not so sure. Every time I see you, you seem concerned about something. I don't know exactly what that something is, but it appears to consume you.

—Nothing consumes me.

—Precisely... That's the point. Nothing is consuming you.

—As I said, everything seems to be about nothing.

—All the fires, the fire. All the rivers, the river. All the shadows, the shadow. Everything is what it ought to be. Take my hand.

I take Carolina's hand and feel her warmth, a warmth that comes from her blood, a blood that circulates inside her body, a body that intersects my life in ways I have yet to understand. I think I need her hand more than she needs mine. She could easily let go of my hand and vanish into that world of hers that does not belong to me, where she exists, and I do not.

The bridge continues to support our bodies. It keeps us above the earth and the river. It provides us with a place of encounter as improbable as the encounters themselves. I come to realize we need this bridge; we need its strength. If the bridge were to crumble, the waters of the river would drag us away. And where would the river take us? If it were to follow its habitual course, the river would not find an outlet since the receiving body of water is absent. Would the river be content to empty itself over a vast desert? A sudden death that would be.

Carolina grasps my hand tightly and raises it up to the sky. She makes a big circle in the air as if wanting to draw the vastness of the universe. She gazes up and around and scrutinizes the confines of the celestial dome above us.

—Everything is what it ought to be. Just look at the sky.

—I see no clouds. It's a bottomless sky.

—It's a perfect sky.

—There's nothing there.

—The problem is that you don't see what's there. It's completely perfect.

—It's a perfect absence. With its pearly-blue tonality, the sky extends in every possible direction. It occupies all the spaces that I cannot touch. It subsumes all other earthbound absences as well. It takes them inside of itself and nourishes them. Yes, it is a perfect sky.

—Where were you before I found you?

—I was at Café Central.

—What were you doing there?

—Drinking a glass of pastis and waiting.

—What were you waiting for?

—I'm not sure. I may have been waiting for Zotikos, or I may have been waiting for myself. In any case, neither of us arrived.

—Let's go back to Café Central, the two of us.

That is not the natural order of things. That space is outside of our communal realm. I suspect Carolina must have seen me multiple times sitting at the table and talking with Zotikos. But she has never ventured to introduce her presence inside that realm. Perhaps she sees it as incompatible with our mutual experience. Or, perhaps, it is Zotikos who she wants to avoid. If that were the case, she then knows that Zotikos is not at Café Central today. She could have placed her hand on my shoulder while I was sitting alone at the table. But the natural order of things is for us to encounter each other at this bridge, over this river. Maybe she wants to be escorted into Café Central, there where I talk about books and nothingness.

With her hand in my hand, I lead the way back to Café Central. Once we arrive, I show her to my customary table and make a sign to Maurice. Unsure of how to proceed this time, Maurice asks us what we want to drink. Carolina says she wants a pastis, which signifies that she intends to understand what truly unfolds in this place. Then she reaches for the portfolio and pulls out the manuscript without first asking.

—So, this is what you were doing for the last few days.

—It isn't finished.

—A book is never finished, correct?

—No, never.

—What's missing?

—That's precisely what the book is about, about what's missing.

—Do you know what that is?

—No, not really.

—So, then you don't know for sure what the book is about.

—That's probably true.

Carolina opens the manuscript and looks through the pages. She finally stops somewhere and reads a passage. Whatever passage she is now reading is coming alive this very moment; it is finally turning into literature. Her face, however, remains passively neutral, showing no emotional response. She then jumps to another page and reads some more. A stillness endures on her face, like the waters of a lake in the morning.

—Does the moon have a mirror?

—It used to have one.

—It must be a rather large mirror.

—Indeed, vast and extensive.

—Could I see my image in that mirror?

—I'm afraid not. The mirror of the moon has vanished.

—How could an immense mirror vanish like that?

—I don't know, but it has.

—Is that what's missing?

—Not only that. Answers are missing, people, words, the fulfillment of expectations.

—Then you have a lot to write about.

She closes the manuscript and returns it to the portfolio. In one sole swig, she empties her glass of pastis. The expression on her face does not change except for the appearance of a dim sparkle in her eyes. Perhaps she wants to say something. But not a word comes out of her mouth. She gets up from the table, turns her back on me, and walks away. In her world, I must have ceased to exist already. In my world, another absence has curdled.

#

He has never spoken about his personal life, Zotikos. Where was he born? Who were his parents? Where does he live? I know as little about him as he knows about me. I know about Laura because I have seen her with him once or twice, not because he tells me about her. He knows about Carolina because I tell him about her, not because he has seen us together. Considering the circles we run around each other, it is not surprising that our personal lives are a great unknown. We seem to exist inside our minds, and what we reveal to each other is only a transactional imperative. However, the quality and depth of those revelations could be extraordinary and beautiful.

At this moment, however, I do want to find him to confirm that he is not forever gone, that his absence is not a definite one. Perhaps he is doing exactly what I was doing last week, hunkered down in his apartment, writing his half of a book about nothing. I hope that he is doing so, indeed. So, I need to find him.

The only people we know in common are Laura and Maurice. Laura is a mystery, I may come across her by chance at the market, or I may not. I have no control over that possibility. Maurice, on the other hand, may know the whereabouts of Zotikos. Perhaps they have a different relationship, a more mundane one. So, when Maurice comes around to serve another table, I grab on to him. He looks surprised and cannot find the words to address me. I begin my quest.

—Today, I'm not staying.

—How come?

—Because I don't want to sit here alone.

—Where's Zotikos?

—I don't know. Have you seen him?

—Not since both of you were here about a week ago.

—Hasn't he come by himself?

—Not at all.

—Do you know where he lives?

—Zotikos? I don't know. I never talk to him.

—You don't know where I live either.

—All I know is that you both live here, right at this table.

Maurice is correct. The life we share with each other has a center, and that center is this very table, now empty. It is from this nodal point that our shared universe branches out. We can only see those branches the other one is willing to illuminate. Then there are the dark ravines inhabited by a legion of unknowns. I do not know about Zotikos precisely what he does not want me to know or what he considers irrelevant, like his home address. But even in this private universe of ours, many areas remain covered by a veil of shadows. What if that is the natural order of things?

I have the option to remain here at the table, drink my pastis, and wait in silence for the eventual arrival of Zotikos. A passive engagement, the road of acceptance. I could also radiate away from this table following one of the illuminated branches as far as possible. I would then be taunting chance, for I may come across Zotikos or fall inside one of those dark ravines. A conundrum. Should an absence be confronted? I have refrained from marching into the desert in search of the mirror of the moon. Neither have I canvassed the village in search of Carolina. Why should I then go searching for Zotikos? Because the accumulation of absences weighs on me? Because I refuse to accept that missing is part of our nature? I cannot tell.

There comes a time when what we know is insufficient, when the risk of the unknown turns sweet and enchanting, when potential losses vanish. Maybe this is such a time. Maybe all I should do is go after that which I miss and hope not to find anything. That hope will protect me from disillusion. If I manage to reverse an absence by reintegrating its presence, then I should celebrate in silence. And if I fail to find what has gone missing, confirming that the absence is real and substantial, then I should weep in silence and bow to the forces of nature.

I do not stay at the table, nor do I drink any more pastis. I simply look ahead and identify an illuminated path that loses itself among the buildings. It shines under a glittering light coming from nowhere. It seems to go far. How far, I cannot tell. But that is the course to follow. So, I venture ahead and accept the path, hoping to find nothing but expecting to be bathed by that glittering light, even if it comes from nowhere.

Inevitably, flowing through the streets brings me in contact with many people. Strangers, most of them. People with whom I share a place and time but whose lives are unknown to me. Each person is an unknown to me, and very likely, each person is an unknown to the other. We weave this matrix of unknowns that hovers over the entire village as we walk and cross each other. We relate to each other in an obtuse way. I doubt the branch I follow is also illuminated for those who walk alongside me. For that to happen, they would have to see the world from the same perspective I do. They would have to be searching for a similar Zotikos. But perhaps that is what we all do, follow the illuminated path.

Ahead of me, a woman and a boy walk holding hands. The boy carries an inflatable pink flamingo much larger than him. They carry on at a comfortable pace, a blissful pace. I follow them at a distance. In the beginning, they share the illuminated path with me, but they soon veer off the path and turn into a street with no glitter. I stop in my tracks. The boy seems content because he wants to climb on top of his pink flamingo and float over the blue above the sand. His illuminated path must be heading in that direction. The boy has hope and the woman, his mother, I assume, wants to indulge him. Her path is illuminated by her caring for the child's happiness. They share their path; they are in harmony. By following them, I would probably reach the shore and be obligated to confront my absence. But what if the child reaches the shore, throws himself into the mirror of the moon, and gets to float on his pink flamingo? In so doing, he would puncture the construct of my absence. But who could guarantee that he will not be disappointed?

On the other hand, by abandoning my illuminated path, the chances of finding Zotikos will be tremendously diminished. The enthusiasm that propelled me to start this venture would be wasted. All I see in this alternative path are shadows, some hope perhaps, but a shadowy hope at best. But hope is a Trojan horse. We let it come inside the confines of our minds where it is certain to unleash disappointment.

Like a stone sculpture, I remain. Let people walk away from me, let time go past me. I do not hear anything, and I have no eyes to see. My skin takes on the rain and the sun and does not wrinkle. I let go by not going. I try not to hope, not to expect. To my right is a boy with a pink flamingo; to my left is the idea of Zotikos. Both propositions are irrelevant at this moment, for I am made of stone.

Chapter Nine

This day is not for searching. The desire to embark on a search for clarification has already damaged me. A search implies that an answer exists somewhere, that with enough courage and determination, that answer will be found. But, unfortunately, I get hurt when I find nothing. And as I have seen lately, nothing is everywhere. Today, thus, I am not searching. But that does not prevent me from venturing out into the world. I can still expose myself to the vagaries of the day without having any agency.

This day is for breathing the loose air without worrying about its salt content. This day is not for chairs and tables. This is not a day for coming or going. If dawn wants to feel like dusk, so be it. If time wants to fall asleep, it can do so. What matters is that nothing matters this day. I can set aside all expectations and accept the nothingness that will ensue without regrets. That is the kind of day this day is.

I do not open the book I am writing. I do not read from any other book. I let language rest for the day. No representations, no signifiers or signifieds. No rhetorical encumbrances, no literary or canonical obligations. I dress lightly and wear no hat. I take no money with me. And once I feel a sincere absence of density, I step out on the street and do not look back.

My initial tendency is to decide in which direction to walk and for what purpose I would do such walking. I am quick to block that thought which lands in my mind right away. The moment the first steps are unchained from compulsory duty, the rest of the steps are free to do as they wish. I am essentially free to meander with no hope guiding my way. At first, I feel a little discombobulated, as if I were to fall into an abyss. But once I get into an agreeable walking rhythm, I feel as if I am floating. I do not turn right or left, nor do I walk up or down stairs. It is the village that approaches me, that turns around me. The buildings parade in front of me, with their windows as eyes and their balconies as smiles.

From this perspective, I can better understand how unexpected things happen. For example, the occasions when Carolina crosses my path—she may have been floating herself while I had an iron grip on the rail of the bridge. If I had let go of the bridge and float like I am now doing, would I have encountered Carolina? Or was she the one who encountered me? That question is valid if one is floating and the other one is not. But, how likely is it for two floating and unexpected paths to cross each other? If there are no expectations, it does not matter if those paths cross each other or not. Expectations weigh us down, even when we are not aware that we are expecting.

Walking without a fixed direction brings me to unfamiliar places, to streets and corners I never visit. It feels as if I am entering a different village. Even people's faces are different in these alien regions, faces unrecognizable to me. I imagine I am unrecognizable to them as well. Unbridled as I am, my steps lead me away from Café Central and certainly away from the shore. An interesting reality that makes me question if I am not somehow directing my steps unconsciously. Perhaps my mind knows where expectations lurk.

Around a corner, under the shade of a stone pine, I come across a restaurant terrace where a few unknown people drink coffee and read the newspaper—a perfect place to breathe the air of this quartier and to observe the life of others. When I sit down at a table, my first instinct is to ask for a glass of pastis. But why introduce such a familiar gesture into this unknown territory? Better to let go of old habits, at least at this moment. So, I order a coffee and a glass of water. Once I am served, I begin to observe everything around me.

People are like any other people elsewhere. Their faces express what they need to express, anxiety, worry, indifference, even joy. But without knowing the private meanings of those expressions, they are like portraits in a museum. I am not related to anyone on this terrace. I am also a portrait which came to sit at a table. If I were to get up and leave at once, I would not forge an absence. We have not spent enough time in each other's presence to engender an absence. A refreshing situation this is for there is nothing to expect.

Not having an expectation does not preclude events from materializing. And that becomes evident the moment Zotikos drops his body on the chair next to me. The spell of unfamiliarity is broken, or so it seems. When I regard him, I notice that his face is the same as before except that he seems calmer, more at ease somehow. He is the portrait of himself but painted by softer strokes. He does not seem surprised to see me. Maybe he is hiding his surprise, or maybe he has been waiting for me. Distancing himself from his habitual silence, Zotikos begins to talk at once.

—You must be looking for something.

—No, I'm not looking for anything.

—Then, why are you sitting at this table under this stone pine?

—I had no idea that this place existed. I just wanted to be among people I don't recognize.

—So, you found what you were looking for.

—You could say so. But I had no expectations whatsoever. I clearly wasn't looking for you.

—I wasn't expecting to find you here either.

—But we are here now.

I believe Zotikos when he says he was not expecting to find me here. He may not reveal everything he thinks, but what he puts into words is always true. Therefore, this circumstantial encounter is not intentionally directed by neither of us. It seems to have happened. But can events just happen like that without an underlying current of causality? I will never be able to answer that question. But we are here now—here we are.

—Zotikos, after about a week of not leaving my

place, I went to Café Central yesterday and found our table empty. You weren't there, and I wasn't there either.

—I know, I haven't been there for a while.

—Why haven't you?

—I've been writing. Writing about *nothing*.

—That's a vast subject. How do you approach it?

—I don't. I just let it approach me. It has the wicked tendency to come around unannounced. Then I struggle to manhandle it.

—What happens then?

—Nothing. That's precisely want happens, nothing. Then I write about it.

He is true to himself, Zotikos. He is also capable of turning a blind eye to situations that impact him emotionally. He knows very well that I reacted to his absence but would not speak about it. Perhaps because that emotion has a presence, and it is not *nothing*. So, I direct his attention back to Café Central.

—I decided not to stay at our table and left right away.

—So, you had expected me to be at Café Central.

—That's entirely possible, even relevant.

—Did you return to your apartment?

—No, I went walking around until I found a child with an inflatable pink flamingo.

—Did you go back to your place then?

—Eventually, I did, but I had to fight against a leaden heaviness that weighed down on me. For a moment, I couldn't move because everything became irrelevant.

—How is it different today?

—I don't expect anything today; I'm just floating.

—Is it relevant that we came across each other unexpectedly under this tree instead of at Café Central?

—We cannot find each other at Café Central because we are both absent from our table at this very moment.

—But we are here now, as you said.

—Yes, we are. Or so it seems.

If Zotikos is writing about nothing, as he says, he is definitely responding to an inner drive demanding satiation. He has a yearning inside, driving him to confront what is not there. He describes it as *nothing*, as if that nothing was made of bone and flesh. His *nothing,* is nothing other than an absence; he just does not see it that way. Nothingness is neutral; it does not imply a loss. And that is why he prefers that term because it shields him from delving into some of his feelings. But in essence, he is doing as I am doing, trying to come to terms with a pruned reality.

—What happened to the child with the inflatable pink flamingo?

—I don't know. Last I saw him; he was heading toward the shore.

—So, he must be floating just like you're floating now.

—Perhaps, if he found what to float on.

—And what are you floating on?

—I'm floating on nothing.

—So, then I should be able to write about what sustains you.

—Are you actually using words in your writing?

—Often, but not always. Sometimes the words fall short of representing what I want to say. Then I write nothing.

—Do you create a space for nothingness to exist?

—Absolutely, there are many blank pages in my manuscript. What's not there is clear to me, but it may not be clear to the reader.

—The reader would then have to pour their own nothingness into those blank pages. The reader is essential. The reader completes the book.

Zotikos does not respond to my assertion; he remains quiet. But that does not mean he disagrees with my observation. He is aware that at some point, I will read whatever he is now writing. Likewise, I know that in due time he will read what I have written. Our parallel manuscripts will converge.

After a long silence, Zotikos summons the waiter and asks for two glasses of pastis. I imagine he wants to make this unexpected encounter feel more familiar. Perhaps he realizes that tangible elements serve as conduits of the mind. The sharing of pastis is not different from the sharing of the soul, nor is it different from sharing a manuscript that contains the soul of a writer. Once we are served, he raises his glass and toasts to all past and future blank pages. I join him in the toast. Then, he starts talking about Laura in the most oblique way.

—There she was for a moment as if she had never left, but when I attempted to touch her, she was no longer.

—Who was she who was not there?

—I could not confirm who she was because she simply vanished.

—Do you know for sure that she was there?

—As sure as I can be of something that is not there.

—You cannot be completely sure; that's the tragedy.

—Not a real tragedy because I had not expected for her to be there at all.

—So, you were expecting nothing.

—Indeed, I was expecting nothing. But that is not what happened. At least for an instant, something must have happened.

—Is *she* the nature of that something?

—There's no way for me to know that. I will never know what I missed.

—Are you disappointed?

—Not necessarily disappointed, but perplexed.

— I'm perplexed, myself, by your lack of understanding.

—What's there to understand?

—Nothing.

And nothing is what we say to each other after that exchange. When we both empty our respective glasses of pastis, Zotikos gets up from the table and regards me with the calm eyes of a true comrade. Unflustered, he turns around and walks away in peace. I watch him disappear among the streets; then I return to my personal universe.

Part Two

A night so long. Endless, it seems. Here I lie immobile, prisoner of short-lived dreams. They pretend to be real, the dreams, but I know very well they have no substance. Nevertheless, they flutter around, taking advantage of my semi-consciousness to mount an extravagant circus. The things they invent, the little monsters; soon, they will be fulminated by the morning light, and I will remember nothing.

What a long night this is! I start to feel warm and toss the bedcovers to the side. The discomfort makes me open my eyes—darkness, darkness everywhere. I am not dreaming this. No, I must be totally awake. I sit on the edge of the bed and confirm that I am awake, indeed. This must be the end of the night, but somehow it is not. All nights come to an end except the very last one. But I am not dead, not yet. So, why this night does not come to an end?

Perhaps the windows refuse to usher in the light of the new day. But there are no shutters or curtains covering my windows; they do not block any light from coming in. They could not keep the day at bay. Neither could they keep the night from entering my room if, indeed, the night is overbearingly present. I step up and approach the window slowly. Yes, the night is still outside. I can see the lampposts trying to fight back the shadows.

I return to my bed and lie down again. Maybe I have not slept for as long as I think. If I close my eyes, I may meet those dreams again. This could be only an interruption, and my sleep will continue to glide until the real morning arrives. I close my eyes; taking in a few deep breaths. I try to fall asleep again. But the same windows that let the night in allow for the street noise to enter as well. There are cars rolling down the street, people talking to each other, a siren far away. Life seems to be palpitating outside as if it were daytime. Perhaps all these sensations are part of a new dream, and I am finally falling asleep. I abandon myself to the possibility of dreaming.

The heat, the noise, the darkness... Sleepless, I open my eyes wide and look at the ceiling: nothing there, a dark field without stars. I turn from one side to the other, and all I see are shadows. Could this be the morning already? Could it be that I am writing about a sleepless night? I cannot tell. What is clear to me is that I am awake and that I am not dreaming. So, what is the point of staying in bed pretending that the night has not ended? If the night has ended, as my body seems to be indicating, I should get up and confront the new day.

I turn on the lights and get dressed. Then I hear the church bells ringing eight times. That sound, which I have learned to ignore out of habituation, now rushes into my consciousness, telling the truth. It reveals that the morning has broken. Time has not stopped, it has continued to flow through the night, bringing me to this morning hour, but it has dragged darkness along with it. There are shadows spilling over everything, flooding what should be an otherwise clear morning. I do not know how to understand this. Either the darkness of the night is eclipsing the morning light, or there is no light this morning, and darkness is the consequence.

I step out of my apartment and descend onto the streets. The lampposts shine brightly, the windows on the adjacent buildings are lit, cars drive by with beaming headlights. The stores are open, people move around in haste, and birds are singing. All seems to indicate that darkness does not matter. An impossible polar night in a meridional village. I study the dark sky attentively, searching for clues. The stars twinkle as usual, but there is no moon. There was a crescent moon last night. Where has it gone? Maybe the moon got confused and changed its phase. Or perhaps the moon is exactly where it should be, but it has nothing to reflect. I should not be concerned with the moon but with the sun instead.

I refuse to consider the possibilities of an overextended night. Perhaps the moon has eclipsed the sun in its entirety, and neither of them is visible. But the temperature has not fallen, and the birds and the animals have not gone quiet. Maybe the sun has fallen below the horizon; maybe it is simply hiding. Or maybe the sun has abandoned its place in the center of our galaxy. Is it possible for the sun to be absent as well? If so, the face of the moon would be as dark as this day. And if the moon had no light on its face, what need would it have for a mirror?

There is no use in getting overwhelmed by what I cannot comprehend. This is not the moment for arresting my life and my writing. This, too, shall pass. If all the absences share a common blood, I would be writing about them all by writing about one. It is in the acceptance of the absence that a presence could be conjured. A body of water, a burning star, a beloved. What sort of presence do they leave behind when they vanish? A memory? And when the memory fades, nothingness?

I return to my apartment, where the manuscript awaits me. As I start weaving words, I do not consider that I am writing during nighttime, for I do not conceive of this day as anything other than daytime. I turn off all the lamps and light a candle. This is the natural order of things.

#

With a final exhalation, the flame dies out. Vigorous darkness surrounds me. In the absence of moonlight, darkness can play as it wishes. Like an unconfined fluid, it glides over every surface, stretching out its territory. It touches everything inside the apartment. I light a match, and the room comes alive again. Quickly, I find another candle and light it before the match expires. I can only see in the presence of light. In the absence of light, my healthy eyes are worth nothing. We are not meant to live in darkness; clearly not. It follows that whatever happened to the sun cannot be construed as a natural event. The absence of the sun is utterly unbearable.

The lifetime of a candle has determined the duration of this writing session. I have written enough for the day or the night. It does not matter which. What matters is that I have struggled to master this situation by means of my words. But how would I know if I have mastered anything? The manuscript needs to be read for it to exist. I need Zotikos for that. Zotikos, in turn, could be immersed in darkness as well this very moment. I would assume so. He must be noticing the invading shadows. He may have ignored the absence of the mirror of the moon, but how could he ignore a never-ending night? He could not.

Enough time has elapsed since I entered my apartment for the earth to cycle around the sun several times. The church bells continue to ring as if nothing has changed. But why bother numbering the passing hours? Twelve, or five, or nine. They become relative numbers with very little meaning. My bodily rhythms are more important; they are totally natural. If I have not slept much, it is because I have not had the need. If I eat, it is because I am hungry. These circadian rhythms do not necessarily obey light and dark patterns. Therefore, does it matter whether we are still circling the sun if it has no direct impact on us? Perhaps I should be more concerned with the impact of a continuous night. Would I respond only to shadows? Would things acquire a softer edge? Would colors lose their preeminence? Would I be blinded by the sun once it returns?

I realize I keep using the word *sun*. I better not name that which is missing for naming it may preclude its return. I do not mention the blue above the sand by name because I hope it will flow back into its bed one day. Likewise, I should be careful not to call the closest star by its name. That is if I expect it will return to shine over us once more. Perhaps a superstition, an attempt to exert some control over ulterior forces. But how else could I deal with the unnatural?

My window offers a picture of the night outside. It is not much different from the night inside. The only advantage inside the apartment is that I control the shadows. Outside on the streets, the shadows are determined by elements out of my control, or maybe by chance. Nevertheless, I need to walk out into the larger night to see how people are managing this situation. I cannot hide inside these walls waiting for the bright star to bathe me with light again.

And so, I enter the exterior night as if I were entering a cave. I prefer to think of the village as being inside a cave because it allows for the continuous existence of the bright star on the outside. It follows that the light does not penetrate this far into the cave, but it does exist in the outside world. Interestingly, nothing seems to have changed in the streets, other than it being nighttime and nighttime only. People seem to go about their lives as if darkness has no bearing on them. They do not seem alarmed or bothered. The lampposts emit enough light to make their lives livable. I imagine rodents are thriving. Not the bats, they need dusk, and dusk is feeble daylight of which we now have none. Darkness also eradicates the intense and disturbing scintillations of certain objects when they reflect light shamelessly. In essence, there is a certain calmness or reduced harshness inside this cave.

Could an absence be both devastating and comforting at the same time? We do accept the absence of the blazing star every evening. Most likely because we are certain the star will reemerge the following day. There is no reason to be anxious; it has returned every day since the world started spinning on its axis. So, perhaps, the comfort I sense, and the equanimity of people in the streets owe themselves to the expectation that this long night will come to an end at some point. To relish on that comfort would certainly protect us from the feelings of devastation. However, that comfort relies on an expectation. And expectations are precisely what I wish to eradicate from my life. It then follows that I cannot accept the comfort because I do not want to be burdened by expectations—a hard choice, that is.

If this were indeed a cave. And this cave was like any other cave; it needs to have an entrance or an opening leading to the world outside. The fact that no light seems to reach the village could be attributed to the village being located at the very end of a rather voluminous and profound cave, far from that opening. Therefore, if I were to walk in the direction of the opening, at some point, the light would become visible. But what direction would that be? Do I need to walk in the dark, not knowing what could befall me? And more complicated, are we actually in a cave?

I meander aimlessly for a while. This should not be any different from walking through the village on a previous regular night. But it feels different; first, there is no moon. However, there are many nights when the moon is not visible. That depends on multiple factors. Therefore, upon further consideration, not seeing the moon is not sufficient to make this a strange night. What is truly different is the number of people on the streets going about their lives. On a regular night, there would be a lot fewer people, and some businesses would even be closed—not tonight. Everything is open, and there is ebullient energy in the air. That could be explained if this were a night of celebration. But this is not a special date, and nothing grandiose has happened.

I wonder if the night is darker at the shore. Would there be synergy if two absences coalesce, that of the crib of all waves and that of the astral galactic epicenter? Would their combined effect be greater than the sum of their separate effects? I wonder if by not having the moon shining over the vast extension of sand, would that expanse resemble a dark lake, calm and indifferent? The only way to know is by exploring, even if we cannot comprehend what we discover.

Like a caravel, I head straight to the shore with whatever little wind I have in my sails. I am not afraid to confront that which disturbs me. I may be disappointed to find precisely what I expect to find. In that case, there would be no discovery. Yet another shortcoming inherent to expectations. So, I carry on hoping for nothing, a hope nonetheless but less magnanimous.

As I begin to approach the shore, the sound of life in the village begins to diminish. Every step I take knocks off a few decibels. By the time I reach the very edge of the shore, a silence reigns supreme. I cannot hear the village, the surf, or the seagulls. Behind me, the scintillating lights of a silent village. In front of me, a darkness whose profundity I cannot fathom.

I venture into the dark lake, but my feet touch no water, for the mirror of the moon is still absent. Up in the dark dome of the sky, the moon is also absent. The stars remain, the far-away ones, but the closest and brightest is absent as well. Perhaps my discovery is that all absences are connected; they may share a common essence—the essence of being longed for.

I have a choice. I could think of this moment as pertaining to daytime and continue to confront the vagaries of the day, or I could think of it as the real nighttime and return to my apartment to rest. Both are valid options. If I were to consider what sort of events may take place while I roam around the dark village or whether I will get any writing done inside my apartment, I would be falling into the trap of expectations once more. Perhaps I should make a choice based on bodily sensations, like how tired I am or if I like a glass of pastis. The problem is that I am not that tired, neither do I crave pastis at this moment. But why do I have to make a choice? Am I expected to choose? Not necessarily. I could decide not to choose anything and simply be. I am just being. More precisely, walking and being since I have left the shore behind me for fear of longing too much.

I realize that longing can install itself in our minds without us being aware. Until this minute, I was unaware that I long for twilight, that battleground were light and shadows struggle for domination. I also long for the smell of saltpeter. There may be many more things I long for without knowing. At least, longing is more acceptable than expecting because it contains no promise. And promises are not what I need at this moment. This is the moment for being.

While in the midst of being, a shadow joins me in my walk. I cannot tell where it came from, nor if it is the shadow of a man or a woman. It is clearly not my shadow, for I have full possession of mine. It follows me in silence. If I stop walking, the shadow stops. If I accelerate my pace a little, the shadow speeds up accordingly. I look all around me, but I cannot see the solid body casting the shadow. The shadow is probably being, just as I am, but does so incorporeally, or so it seems. I try to listen for someone else's steps, but I hear nothing, nothing, nothing. Could nothingness cast a shadow? I think it could. Zotikos is already experimenting with nothingness as literature. And literature is nothing but the shadow of our lives.

The shadow then moves past me. It quickly begins to gain some distance. It is my shadow, then, that follows the silent one. I cannot let it vanish, for I would probably long for its company and silence. So, I pick up my pace. In tandem, we traverse streets, turn corners, and dodge some other shadows. Our angles change in response to the light shed by the lampposts. Sometimes the shadows lean acutely and grow long. Other times they stand up like dark soldiers. We then turn into a street that becomes narrower and narrower until it finally comes to a dead end. I see both shadows projected on the wall at the end of the street. I recognize the other shadow, the dark silhouette of Carolina. I am not prepared for the darkness of this reality, so I turn around and run away in the only possible direction there is—back into the night.

Alone, with no contours next to me, I penetrate the penumbra of the village. I proceed at a slow pace, the pace of those who do not expect to get anywhere. And that is precisely how I feel, unencumbered by expectations. At this rhythm, I can scrutinize the dark façades of the buildings, the doors, windows, the benches in the park, the somber trees and their leaves, everything that stands quietly and abandons itself to being observed. All elements are thoroughly bathed in fluid darkness—a tinge that does not change their essence but their appearance. Darkness makes all elements resemble each other by stripping them of their natural color. What replaces the color is a certain shade of nothingness. These shades of nothingness, variable as they may be, share an absence of color. By walking among the shadows, through the streets of a village dilapidated of its color, I am surrounded by a rather large absence. However, the absence of color is not absolute, unlike that of the crib of all waves or that of the ball of fire. This is a partial absence, for sometimes the lampposts illuminate a certain green on a wall or the remains of redness on a door.

A partial absence is somehow more brutal than an absolute one. That is because in being partial, this absence contains remnants of that which is no longer. Those remnants hurt as much as a sad reminiscence or an uncomfortable dream. It may be easier to forget what we no longer have because our memories become feeble with time. But the continuous faded presence of a larger absence is intolerable. At the same time, the glimmer of a presence may provide hope for the return of that which has gone absent. Perhaps daytime will follow this long night and illuminate the return of the caravels.

There may be no use in walking errantly through the streets in the village when reconciliation with my reality can only happen upon self-reflection and writing. Self-reflection I can do anywhere, right here in the shadows of this very moment. But writing requires the solitude of my apartment, where it matters very little if daytime follows the night or if the night has no followers. That is where the words and ideas need to be born. That is where the concept of an absence, total or partial, will need to emerge. Once the interior battle has been rendered on the page, I will have completed my duty to uncover, reveal, and illustrate. Then it would be up to the reader to bestow the book with flesh and bones and breathe life into it. I cherish the mind of my accomplice.

#

Inside the confines of my apartment, I feel relatively intact. The external world, ebullient with reality, cannot easily penetrate this ambit. Of course, there are the windows ready to open up to the world with their relaxed voyeuristic attitude, but I could close those at any time. Here, I am free from encumbrances, primarily those of nature. The only natural element that imposes any order is my own freedom. I am free to do as I wish inside this apartment. At least, I think so, even if that is not completely true. The truth is that here is where I write. And that is a certain freedom, if not an absolute one.

The manuscript that I have been working on rests on its back. It does not reveal any signs of wanting to be read. It sleeps unmolested. Not having a conscience of its own, it harbors no expectations. It does not await interpretation, for that is not in its nature. I am intimately related to the manuscript, as any giver of birth can be, but the manuscript does not reciprocate the feeling. That does not mean that the manuscript rejects me. No, it could not do that. After all, what the manuscript contains are only words. And words have no meaning of their own. The reader will aggregate all those dormant words and attribute meaning. If that meaning relates to my intentions at the time of writing, then my job would be complete. But I should have no urgency in writing because, if I did, it would create an expectation.

I expect nothing. I expect nothing at all. Well, that is not entirely true. I feel at peace inside my apartment because I expect the outer world to remain outside. I take on writing because I expect the words to behave well and express my ideas. Somehow, I have the expectation that the sand at the shore will be once again covered by the blue that is now missing, that the caravels will be able to float and return, that the moon will see the reflection of the light that is reflected on its face. I expect this night to come to an end. I also expect to come across Carolina on a more luminous path.

By harboring all these expectations, I am opening the door to multiple disappointments. These disappointments could, in turn, introduce sorrow into my life. Sorrow is not what I yearn for. It then follows that those expectations need to be eviscerated, emptied of their stinging venom, and rendered flat and lifeless. The only way to accomplish that is by writing about them. In so doing, I would have the chance to defang and defeat the expectations. However, I must write without wanting to write. The paragraphs could not have an ulterior motive other than being agglomerations of words occurring at any given time for no reason. That is, it must not matter what I write about.

I sit at my desk and open the floodgates. The words

are free to parade as they wish. I am intent in not having an intent. Let the writing write itself. It does not matter. But as soon as the first few words make their entry, the doorbell rings. Is the doorbell ringing as part of the story, or is the doorbell ringing for real? I listen carefully, and the doorbell rings again. There is no doubt; someone is at the door. But I do not expect anyone. Nobody should be ringing at my door in the middle of this never-ending night. I am a person of no consequence. If I do not answer, the ringing will eventually come to a stop. I focus my attention on writing a few more words and manage to finish a paragraph. When I read the full paragraph, I realize that I wrote about someone ringing a doorbell and someone else not answering the ringing. This is not possible. I will not permit reality to force its way into my writing, especially not in this surreptitious way. On the other hand, if it does not matter what I write, then reality does not matter either. The doorbell rings once more.

I get up from my desk and make it to the door. I will open the door. I will confront a presence that I am not expecting. There may be a reason for such a presence. And if there is none, it would not matter. But if there is a reason, it may not matter either. However, I do not open the door at once. I wait a moment to confirm that the person on the other side of the door still wants to come inside. If that is the case, I will hear the doorbell again. If silence is what I hear, then the person's intentions are not that strong, and it will not matter much if I answer the door or not—the doorbell rings.

When I open the door, I find myself in front of a completely unexpected presence. Here she is, Carolina, illuminated by the dim light that escapes through the door. She exudes the calmness appropriate to her usual self. And with ease, she lets herself inside the apartment. She obviously expected me to open the door. For what other reason would she have rung the bell? But I thought she did not know where I lived. I clearly do not know where she lives. She, on the other hand, has found me. How did that happen? Perhaps she wanted to find me and followed my trace. But if she went looking for me, she must have had me as a constant object in her mind. That object constancy proves that I exist in her world, even in my absence. I thought I vanished completely from her mind when we go our separate ways. Maybe this long night is difficult for her.

She begins to wander inside the apartment. Into every room, she goes as if exploring a cave. I follow her in silence. She opens the closets and the drawers; she looks inside the kitchen. She stands in front of my bookshelf and studies the titles. She then picks Rilke's *The Notebooks of Malte Laurids Brigge*, the same book that Zotikos was reading a while back, and opens it on a seemingly random page. She begins to read.

— *In one's mind, there must be regions unknown, meetings unexpected and long anticipated partings, to which one can cast back one's thoughts.*

—I wasn't expecting to meet you here in my apartment.

—Neither was I until I rang the doorbell.

—What brought you here?

—You brought me here. Or perhaps an unknown region of your mind called upon me.

—There are many of those regions. I couldn't count them.

—One of those regions leads you on nighttime walks.

—All the walks I take are nighttime walks. There are no others to be had.

—Why do you follow shadows?

—I only follow the shadows that follow me.

—That's a sure way of getting nowhere.

She is correct. My walks lead me to dead ends. I walk and follow shadows in the thick of this endless night, and nothing follows from that. I cannot grab those shadows; they are in themselves immaterial. However, in the shadow I followed, I think I recognized her materiality. Maybe an unknown region in my mind wanted that shadow to be hers. That region needs to believe that I exist in her world, even in my absence. But maybe I only began to exist when we crossed our paths in the middle of the night. The shadow sprung on me. It was not my shadow that surprised the other one. Her shadow found mine, and only then did I begin to exist for her. I am certainly getting nowhere.

—I've been writing with no intent.

—And how does that feel?

—It's rather liberating. I'm trying to toss away all expectations. The words would need to decide on how to come together to create meaning.

—Do they manage to create anything at all?

—I don't know yet.

—But do you believe words will form alliances and create a communal meaning? Isn't that an expectation?

—I don't expect any specific meaning. It's up to them to decide what to mean and then for the reader to interpret such meaning.

—So, you don't know what you're writing about.

—I don't really know. However, I'm influenced by what's missing around me.

—Then you're writing about shadows.

—Not about shadows. They're cast by material entities. I'm writing about absences. And those absences are cast upon us for no apparent reason. They lack materiality and a reason to exist.

—How do you know if those absences exist as you claim they do?

—I may know when I finish writing about them.

Carolina becomes silent, and her calm expression hardens just slightly. She returns Rilke's book to its proper place on the bookshelf. With the same ease with which she entered the apartment, she makes it back to the door. She then joins the night outside. A parting I may have anticipated.

#

My body tells me it must be noontime, a fact I cannot confirm in the absence of the ball of fire. I have no need for sleep, but I crave food and drink. If I do nothing about those needs, they may exchange places after a few hours. Those essential rhythms are now beginning to lose their way. That happens because the hours seem not to count anymore. They may count in a mathematical sense as a measure of the passage of time, but they are disentangled from the rhythms of daily life. Why not follow my bodily needs regardless of when they occur in this dayless night?

My body craves food and drink, but my spirit craves an exchange of the minds. To satisfy my cravings, I will have to venture into the night once more. There is nothing to fear in the outside world. I am certain to find the same village, albeit flooded by darkness. Not an evil darkness, for it has no mind of its own nor a body. This darkness results from the unavailability of light. So, it is born out of an absence. Its existence is contingent upon the absence of another entity, the ball of fire in this case, so it can mean no evil of its own. Reassured,

I obey my cravings and step out into the dark village.

The streets are almost deserted of people. If this were indeed noontime, many more people would be coming and going. This might as well be midnight. Perhaps people have lost track of their daily rhythms and go out on the street when they need to, not when the clock strikes twelve times. There may be birds flying in the sky, but I cannot see them. And I do not know if the cats I see are of the nocturnal kind. Have they changed their habits? This absence touches everything, and everything needs to accommodate itself to its presence.

Even if time is not of the essence, there is no reason to delay the satiation of my cravings. So, I head for Café Central, hoping that it will be open, lit, and that Zotikos will be sitting at our table. I wonder what he would say about this extended night. I wonder if he may even recognize it. If he is molested by the darkness, he may exalt the beauty of light at noontime.

Turning the habitual corner brings me in full view of Café Central. The place is open and lit by various chandeliers and small candles on each table. I can recognize Maurice tending to a small number of patrons. And at our table, a man wearing a hat sits reading a book. The brim of the hat casts a shadow on the man's face preventing me from recognizing who he is. But by his gesture when turning a page of the book and when drinking some clear liquid out of a glass, I know it must be Zotikos.

Through the shadows into the light, I advance. Reaching the table, pulling out a chair, and sitting down is easy. The difficult part is confirming the identity hidden under the brim of a hat on this man's tilted head. He continues to read his book and does not look up to acknowledge my arrival. This being as pure a gesture as only Zotikos can perform, I conclude that is him. And, indeed, when the man looks up, the brim of the hat revealing his face, I find myself in front of Zotikos, just as I had expected.

This time I was not disappointed, for the face hidden by the brim of the hat is that of Zotikos. However, if what I really expected was for this to be another person usurping our table, then I would have been disappointed. Furthermore, I would have had to explain why I came to sit at the table without asking for permission in the first place. This is not what happened.

After having revealed his face, Zotikos tilts his head

and returns to his book without offering a greeting or any other word whatsoever. This behavior, as well as the gestures that accompany this behavior, are quintessential Zotikos. Everything in Café Central is as I know it, except for the darkness outside and the many lights inside. Maurice is like himself, and as such, he now brings me a glass of pastis. The only element that I cannot explain is the hat on Zotikos' head. Without a ball of fire up in the sky, there is no practical reason to wear a hat. There is no need to cover any brightness because all we have is darkness. Zotikos is not fond of fashion, so this is not a fancy of his. He must have other reasons.

My first inclination is to inquire nonchalantly about the hat. Nevertheless, I refrain myself. What matters most is not a simple oddity like the hat but the overall status of Zotikos as a writer dealing with difficult issues that he does not want to unravel. He comes to this table for a reason, to commune with me. Likewise, I seek an exchange when I come to this table. We may be following different paths, but our purposes are not so divergent. We both search for an explanation by means of thoughts and words, even when we fail to utter a word to each other, as we are doing this very moment.

But Zotikos knows that I am here and that I will listen and read his words whenever he decides to share them with me. I know he is here and will do likewise. This is the field of words. And therefore, we return to our table, whether day or longest night.

—May I ask what you're reading?

—Certainly, feel free to ask me.

—Then, what are you reading?

—A book of no consequence.

—Of no consequence in general, or, of no consequence to you?

—What is the difference?

—You, as Zotikos, are a unique reader. It could be that your rendition of the book doesn't please you. However, the rendition of the book by another reader may be pleasing to him or her.

—Even if we're reading the same paragraphs and sentences?

—Precisely.

—Then, this book is of no consequence to me. But I already knew that. And if it were of consequence to another reader, in what way would that change my own experience?

—You would be confronting plurality.

—So, how many readers are there?

—I don't know, Zotikos. But tell me, how many nights are there?

—There's only one night that gets interrupted by brief periods of daylight. For example, it is nighttime now, and we're waiting for daylight to interrupt the night's flow.

—Is that why you're wearing that hat?

—You can never be sure when daylight will strike.

Never a direct response. He is compelled to circle around questions for which he has no answers. Zotikos is clearly experiencing this night in his own personal way. As such, his reaction is original and would not relate to mine. He knows it is nighttime, and he serves himself of the chandeliers and candles to read his book. But he does not seem to be affected by the absence of the burning star that should come to interrupt this night. He simply accepts the night as it is and passively waits for things to take a different turn. Perhaps that is how he handles Laura's absence. He knows she is no longer with him, but the flow of that situation could, at some point, be interrupted. I cannot tell if he harbors that expectation. I cannot tell if he would be disappointed if Laura were never to return. What I am certain about is that he will not tell me.

— Zotikos, the other night, or this one since there is only one according to you, I came across a passage by Rilke where he talks about the unknown regions in our mind.

—Does he claim to know what those are?

—No, he makes no such claim. But I was wondering if you think regions like that exist in your mind.

—By virtue of them being unknown, how could I know about them?

—You may not know what they contain, but you could be aware of their existence. Like you're writing a book about nothing but still writing a book.

—What makes you believe that I'm writing a book?

—You mentioned that yourself a few days ago, didn't you?

—Yes, but the writing flow could have been interrupted.

—Has it been interrupted?

—I'm not sure. If time goes by and I fail to add another word to my book about nothing, then it may seem that the flow has been interrupted. The question is, for how long do I have to wait without writing a single word about nothing to know for sure that the flow has been, indeed, interrupted?

—Zotikos, I don't know the answer to that question.

—I don't know it either.

Perhaps the best approach is not to approach him at all. If I take a step forward, he retracts. If I move to the right, he moves to the left. Zotikos does not allow for proximity. He wants to engage, but he does that only on his terms. He avoids answering me directly when I ask direct questions. He has clear feline tendencies. So, there is no point in calling him because he will never respond. There is no point in pressing an argument because he will dodge it. But despite those peculiar habits, he returns, over and over, to this table where he probably feels understood.

He saw with his own eyes that the blue above the sand is no longer at the shore. He did not acknowledge having seen that, but I am certain that it made an impression on him. And that impression, even if he does not share it with me, must be lodged somewhere inside his mind. Also, this period without Laura must have had a serious impact on him, but he chooses not to talk about it. And I am certain that he does not take lightly the absurd prolongation of this night. He could not ignore the presence of those absences. Perhaps he accepts them. Thus, he tames their devastating force.

Is it possible for a person to accept the outcome of an event but harbor expectations that such an outcome will be a different one? Probably not if the acceptance is genuine. Perhaps, then, full acceptance could be the antidote to expectations. And once a person is free from the weight of expectations, there will be no disappointments. I will bring up this subject with Zotikos as indirectly as I can.

—You see, Zotikos, even while moonless, this is a beautiful night.

—Yes, I agree. We don't need the moon.

—It seems that without the moon, the night can be whole, undiluted.

—Let's not have the moon anymore.

—Wouldn't you miss it?

—I'm not missing it now; why would I miss it later?

—Because your sense of beauty could change once this night is over.

—But this night isn't over yet.

—Would it ever be over?

—How could I know the answer to that question?

—Don't you expect for this night to die away?

—A night like this one should be cherished and preserved. It may never die away.

—Zotikos, you cannot expect that.

—I don't know what to expect. Things are what they are. All I know is that it is nighttime and that the moon is not showing its face. What else is there to know?

—As you just said, how could I know the answer to that question?

He tilts his head, and the brim of the hat casts a shadow again. Immersed in his reading, Zotikos becomes silent. He is not one to pose many questions. And when it comes to responding to questions, he shows his feline qualities and turns away from the subject. I am certain that he thinks deeply about what I ask him, plus he must be entertained with his own dilemmas as well. He writes his thoughts down, but I do not what he writes about.

#

The night has nowhere to go. Without the intervention of the ball of fire, it is bound to exist eternally. Maybe the night is the essence of the universe, the glue that binds everything together. A star can burst and turn into gas and disappear. But the night has nowhere to go, it is just there. I shall do as Zotikos and accept it for what it is, at least for the moment.

After not speaking for a while, Zotikos decides to take leave from Café Central. He signals his desire by emptying the glass of pastis, closing the book he has been reading, and standing up. He does not have the habit of saying goodbye, probably because our exchange continues uninterrupted in his mind. Or perhaps because saying goodbye introduces a certain vulnerability. It is also implicit that we will reconvene at the same table at some point in the future. Precisely at what point in time is never stipulated. In that sense, we give each other the impression of not having an expectation of the encounter, but deep inside, we both count on it. Otherwise, why do we keep on coming to the same table at the same café?

This time, however, I will not lose sight of Zotikos

as he marches away. He will most likely go to where he lives, to where he writes. I do not care for knowing where he lives, but I need to find out what he is writing about. He must be struggling with all the absences, those we share and those particular to him. And just as I am doing, he must be processing those absences by writing about them. He cannot help it; he has the disease within him.

I wait until he gains some distance from Café Central to start following him. With darkness as my ally, I shall stay invisible and discrete. The first streets he traverses are known to me, a common ground. But he soon starts veering toward the areas of the village I rarely visit. As we turn corners and follow streets, in tandem but not in mutual awareness, I begin to recognize the neighborhood as the one where we once met by accident. Or perhaps it was not by accident that he dropped on the chair next to me unannounced. I may have ventured into his world without knowing, and naturally, he did not make me aware of that. Whether this is his world or not, I am not sure, but the restaurant terrace into which he is heading is the one where he materialized that one time. The stone pine stands tall as in the previous occasion but casts no shade in this long night. And it is this tree I use to abscond my body. This is the first time I observe Zotikos while existing outside of my presence. This is Zotikos unknown.

He greets nobody and promptly sits at a table where he proceeds to open his book and starts to read without removing his hat. I recognize every one of his gestures; he does not produce new ones. When a waiter brings him a glass of clear liquid that appears to be pastis, I realize that Zotikos is being himself—just elsewhere. This train of events, however, can change at any time. If I expect that he would do something drastically different from what he does in my company, I would be fooling myself. Likewise, if I expect that he would just recycle all gestures and engage in the same activities, I would also be fooling myself. Better not to expect anything. Perhaps this is not his world, as I may have thought, and he is just passing by. However, the waiter knew what to serve him without him ordering anything. This must then be at least a part of his world.

Time goes by. I know not how much, but it does go by. Nothing exceptional happens as Zotikos continues to read and drink. The only aspect of this situation that differs from Café Central's is that Zotikos remains alone. He does not talk to anyone, and nobody comes to talk to him. This sole experience may not be sufficient to label him as a loner, but it would not surprise me that he is one. But when he is at Café Central, is he not a loner then? He could just be a loner who happens to be in my presence. Yes, I do speak to him, and he responds. But he rarely starts the dialogue. Plus, he never reveals a need for my presence. Is he capable of revealing anything at all?

The fact that I am watching from behind a tree trunk implies that I expect to discover something about Zotikos' behavior that I do not know. Since I know so little, almost anything new he does would be a discovery. However, I could be wasting my time by harboring such expectations. What matters to me is not what he does but what he does not tell me.

All at once, Zotikos closes the book, gets up, and drops a few coins on the table. It seems the pattern of behaviors I have come to know so well is about to change. Without saying goodbye to anyone, he leaves the terrace and ventures once more into the streets. To follow him is to assert my need for discovery and to yield to the pressure of expectations. Not to follow him is to accept this night for what it is, a prolonged darkness.

He walks with his head hanging down. Either he is absorbed in thought, or he cares not for what surrounds him. Or perhaps he is being careful not to stumble while walking in the dark. I doubt that he cares much for his surroundings. He did not react to the vastness of the desert at the shore when it was in plain sight, right in front of him. If he had a reaction, he kept it buried inside of him. At some point, however, that inner vessel where he stores all those reactions is bound to overflow. And then what happens?

If this were to be the neighborhood where he lives, we should have already arrived at his apartment. But he keeps on walking, and his direction is now questionable. We are not heading back toward Café Central, neither are we staying in this unknown area. Could it be that he knows that I am following him? He could be leading me on an erratic walk to confuse me, to hide where he lives. But that is unlikely since it is rather dark, and I have kept my distance. Maybe he walks all day instead of writing that book he claims to be writing. Perhaps that is what he means when he says that he is writing about nothing. He may be, indeed, writing nothing.

We come upon a plaza where the lampposts are so numerous and luminous that it seems like daylight. The plaza is as bright as it is empty. Maybe this is the relic of a typical night, and everyone is asleep. I cannot tell. He slows down his pace and slumps his body on an empty bench bathed by the light of a lamppost. I remain in the shadows of the plaza perimeter, observing him. So much light raining on Zotikos, and so much I have yet to illuminate about him. But I do not expect these lights will reveal much; they cannot shine inside of him.

He then brings the book out and begins to read once more. The brim of the hat invites shadows that fall all over his face. His face, thus, vanishes. From where I stand, I see his illuminated figure, reading but miss his facial gestures. His body seems to be in peace. His mind, I know not. For a while, he continues reading until the moment he closes the book and lays it down next to him on the bench. He looks ahead of him and remains immovable. I wonder if he is thinking about what he just read or whether he is trying to understand why the night surrounds this island of light.

Zotikos then gets on his feet. He leaves the book on the bench and starts walking in my direction. Perhaps he does know that I am following him and wants to confront me. I retreat and find cover inside in a dark portal. When he reaches the plaza's perimeter, he does not walk toward where I am hiding, nor does he go back to retrieve his book. He simply embarks on his walk again with his head hanging down.

I wonder what sort of book he was reading. I also wonder why he abandoned the book. He must have liked the book because he seemed to be reading with intensity. If so, what compelled him to leave it behind? Maybe he left the book on the bench to entice my attention, knowing that I would probably be interested in the book. This, of course, could only be the case if he knew that I am following him. Or perhaps this is how he treats all books once he is finished reading them. If that were the case, his apartment would not contain a single bookcase since he would have no need for storing books already read.

I could go and retrieve the abandoned book. But if

I do, I will lose track of Zotikos, who is already gaining distance from me. There is no time to satiate both curiosities. The book is static; it will not move on its own. I can always return to this plaza and collect the book later if nobody else snatches it before me. Zotikos, however, is in full motion and will soon vanish if I do not move along with him. So, I resume my tracking of Zotikos at a safe distance.

It appears that his walk is a random one. If he were intent in reaching a specific destination, he would not be making so many turns. And the more turns he makes, the more it seems to me that he is walking in a large circle. Maybe he has a hard time making his way in this darkness. Or maybe he is clearly aware that I am following him and is looking for an opportunity to confuse me and break away from my chase. Regardless of his walking antics, I am determined to find out more about him. So, I continue my pursuit.

After some confusing roundabouts, he stops turning as often and appears to be following a clear direction. This certitude is accompanied by a hastening in his pace. He is not running, but he is walking much faster. I keep up with him and cut through the veil of the long night. It soon becomes clear that he is heading for the shore. If we continue in this direction, we will inevitably arrive at the scene of the absence. He knows where he is going. And perhaps he knows that I am going there with him. And soon enough, the inevitable materializes.

I did not expect to face this vast absence at the shore in the middle of this long night. But Zotikos has brought himself here and me along with him. Without the moon, the black desert has no beginning and no end. It seems as if the world ceases to exist, as if an endless fall is certain for those who venture beyond the shore. And Zotikos must feel the same, for he stops walking. He then takes a few steps along the sidewalk and comes to the door of a building standing in front of the shore. He lets himself in through the door and closes it behind him. After a couple of minutes, light shines through a window on the third floor, and I discern the shadow of Zotikos looking out. He knows about the absence. He is a witness to it.

\#

What matters is not what we know but what we do with that knowledge—provided, of course, that we abide by an action imperative. However, if we are not obligated to act, knowledge could remain locked inside our minds and retain its action potential. Zotikos knows the caravels cannot return because they have nothing on which to float. He has not shared that knowledge with me. Somehow, he does not feel an obligation to bring that devastating reality into our shared universe. Perhaps he is afraid of its monstrosity, or maybe he is completely untouched by it. He must be equally aware that this night keeps on getting longer and longer. From that same window where he now stands facing the shore, he could ascertain not only the absence of the mirror of the moon but of the moon itself. And if like myself, he was to expect a breaking morning, he must be aware that it is now long overdue.

I will not confront him. To what avail? He has chosen to keep that knowledge inside his mind for some reason. A reason unknown to me but I assume necessary for him. He must be processing those absences in his own private way, which may turn out to be like my own approach. Yes, he could be writing precisely about the blue above the sand and the burning star, but not about his yearning for Laura. Or maybe he is writing about each of those absences. At the same time, he could be writing about none of them and thus the nothingness he refers to. Regardless of the way in which he is dealing with his knowledge, I am almost certain he will not reveal much in our conversations. And that is why I will not confront him.

I better leave the shore, for no answers will be found at this moment. All I can rely on are questions, silence, and a mounting sense of expectation. The latter I should avoid at all costs. So, I turn my back on the shore and direct my steps toward the village where the shadows are vibrant. The streets receive me, not with glory, but with the kindness of acceptance. The village has no will of its own. It dons the cloak of darkness if no daylight is to be had; it is oblivious to the sound of the waves lapping its shore; it cares not for who traverses its streets. This village is also a witness to the absences, but it is unmindful of them.

I have come to know of two devastating changes to the natural order of things. I did not purposely seek that knowledge, but I now possess it. And just as those events occurred without my direct intervention, other equally devastating events may ensue. That may augment my knowledge base, even if that is not what I am after. Yes, what matters is not what we know but what we do with that knowledge. What I do, I do with words.

Every one of my steps creates a sound. The streets do not react to the nature of the sound even when they are accomplices in their production. Stepping on gravel produces a raspy sound that is completely missing when I step over asphalt. Over grass, my steps acquire a moist thump. The echo produced by these sounds varies in relation to the width of the streets and the height of the adjacent buildings. The interaction of the sole of my shoes and all those physical elements creates the sound of my steps. The night and the village accept all the sounds on equal terms and are not interested in changing them. Should I not do likewise? If I were to forget that there was once a burning star to put the night to rest and a body of water at the shore, would I attain the peacefulness of the streets?

Perhaps the elements that I now miss have not disappeared at all. They could have become imperceptible to me, giving the impression that they have vanished.

If I were to walk softly, taking care to place one foot after another with utmost care and delicacy as to not produce any sound, would my steps disappear? I think not. The steps would still be happening, but they would be imperceptible. I could make it all the way to my apartment without the streets noticing me. Perception could have tricked me. This night may not be that long. It may have been interrupted by the emergence of the burning star without me noticing. I may be blind to the day. And at the shore, perhaps the crib of all waves has not become sterile as I think. I may not be sensing the waves. However, I perceive everything else around me, so why would I miss only those two elements? Do I perceive everything else around me? I cannot tell.

I realize that missing the mirror of the moon has forced me to consider it with more force and urgency than when it was present. Its absence has made it brutally essential, and to some extent, even palpable. I have walked along the shore multiple times without noticing the vastness of the body of water. But now that it has vanished, its absence makes it seem infinitely present. Likewise, the unending night makes the absent day even more brilliant and encompassing. Their unavailability makes them magnanimous. Or perhaps my expectation of a future reencounter is what alters their essential physical condition. Here again, perception may be playing a trick on me. By not having a perception of the missing element, my imaginary perception, afflicted by expectations, is running amok. Better then to keep walking through the village in the middle of this night with sonorous or quiet steps. Better to move away from the waves that lap at the shore, or not, toward the safety of my apartment where the unformed words await me.

Arriving at my abode unleashes the possibility of discovery. Not of the physical world, for that is what happens on the streets, but of the unseen world that resides inside my mind. It is there, in the world of thoughts, that I need to do the work of discovery. Once I succeed in formulating and processing the natural order of my absences, I would be ready to reconcile it with the natural order of things in the physical world. What is the use of running out to the shore just to confirm that physical elements are absent? What I am left with is nothingness, and nothingness has no physicality. Likewise, looking up to the purple depths of the night only confirms that it is endless. I cannot touch it with my hands. The knowledge that I seek can only be obtained by reflecting on the meaning of the various absences. And the only way to find meaning is by writing about what I am trying to understand. There is only one way, the way of the manuscript.

I return to the manuscript, hoping to ignite the words, to set them in motion, to be surprised by their revelations. However, when I read what I last wrote, I find it confusing and not necessarily illuminating. When I wrote those words, it is possible that they meant something different to me than what they mean now. Or maybe the long night is dulling my senses. I could also be a different person now from the one who wrote the last paragraphs. But if that were the case, once I finish the manuscript, it will be incomprehensible even to myself. This manuscript needs to coalesce with that of Zotikos to find its ultimate form and meaning. In the meanwhile, I must trust the process and proceed with the discoveries.

Have I indeed lost something? Do I truly feel that something I possessed or enjoyed has disappeared from my life? I could say that youth has disappeared forever.

But that is a relative term for nobody knows with any certainty when youth ends. Therefore, I could not say that I have lost my youth. Have I then lost the possibility to see the return of the caravels? Have I lost the joy in seeing the face of the moon reflecting light in the middle of the night while the moon sees its own reflection on that mirror that serves to support the returning caravels? I may not have lost those experiences; they are just not taking place at this moment. Yes, they are absent. But so is Carolina. She is absent at this very moment. However, I have not lost the hope that we will see each other again at some point in the future. So, why is that absence less painful? Perhaps because it is a recurrent one, a loss that strikes over and over, thus losing its potency. If I were to miss the crib of all waves or the ball of fire on a regular basis, would I end up accepting their absences and consequently attaining a moderate degree of contentedness? Maybe the uniqueness of an absence makes it seem more terrifying.

I could define something by accentuating everything that is not that something. For example, I could define the earth by writing about the entire solar system up to the very edge of the atmosphere and stopping right there. By not including the earth in my writing, I would have defined it. If I were to write about hate, love would be implicit. If we find a closed door, we wonder what is behind it. If somebody covers our eyes, we will struggle to see. This may be what Zotikos is doing. By writing about nothing, he is writing about everything.

I should follow the edge of the absence without entering its realm. Even if the absence is immense, it must have a natural edge that separates it from that which is not absent. That edge is sure to give the absence a form. But where to find the edge? The shore is an edge, not precisely demarcated, but an edge, nevertheless. But what is the edge of the night? It cannot be dusk because dusk is a transition, thus relative and incorporeal. Nobody can touch dusk as nobody can touch the edge of a wave. What would be the edge of an encounter with Carolina? When she departs and waves goodbye? What if her perfume remains floating in the air after she has vanished? I could not touch that either.

Without a particular intention, setting aside all expectations, accepting the possibility of an incomprehensible result, I sit down and continue to work on my manuscript. I will not write about what is not there but about what I think is there, thus somehow defining the very absences that afflict me. The words will pave the way; they will mold themselves around the voids and penetrate those porous and intangible edges. And without them knowing, the words will delineate the very curvature of an absence.

Chapter Eleven

A thousand and one nights or only forty; I cannot tell. I have written for a long time. Without the intromission of daylight, time becomes insubstantial. It becomes ethereal; it leaks away unnoticed and leaves no trace of its flow. This long night is not static; some of its qualities change gradually, like the lightness of the air or the appearance of a previously unseen star. This night, however, cannot be divided into discrete quanta of time. How to decide on the precise moment when a night ends, and another one begins? What difference would it make? Let the night behave as it wishes.

The accumulation of words suggests that I have written much. Perhaps there are hidden answers in the text. If there are such answers, I clearly know not where they are. I have a sense of what the text means, but not a complete one. There is only one imperative: to write and hope for the mind to insert itself between the crevices of the absences and perform its discoveries.

I feel the temptation to read what I wrote in the last segment of this unending night. But I soon refrain from such vain exercise. What would the purpose be? To feel that I am approaching a certain understanding of what is not there? That will only provide me with a partial meaning. Even worse, that partial meaning could have an impact on what I will write next, thus introducing lies into the text. No, I will not read anything until I am finished with the manuscript. But how would I know that I am finished? When there is no more angst left inside of me, or when this night finally comes to an end? I do not know, and it does not matter. Let the writing behave as it wishes.

I wish, however, for an encounter with Carolina to take place, not by chance but by design. To me, they seem to happen only by chance and by chance only. But I suspect that for Carolina, our rendezvous are not fortuitous. I sense that she orchestrates them with delicate precision. Could I *will* an encounter without her predetermined interest? That is, could I insert myself into her reality without being summoned? If that were possible, I would be bringing her temporary absences to an end. There would be consequences, both for her and me. For me, it would mean the fulfillment of a wish and the apparent mastery of an absence. But for her, it could be devastating. She would be confronting a reality for which she is not prepared. Removing the veil of chance may also expose the materiality of her vanishing self. But why would I not honor my wish when almost everything else is out of my hands? So, I leave the writing aside and take to the night and the streets in search of an encounter with Carolina. Let chance behave as it wishes.

I welcome the shadows and the anonymity they provide. I do not want to be noticed. I do not want to be heard. I do not want to be thought about. I care not to step hard on the hard ground since I aim for silence. I want to glide as a translucent nothingness, porous and diaphanous. If I cannot be perceived, I could not be expected. I must appear from the shadows, from non-perception to being perceived. How else could I guarantee to be the initiator of an encounter?

Where could Carolina be? In her world devoid of my existence, or in the world that contains both of us? I only know of the world where we coincide. The other one is only a concept for me but a reality for her. Or so, I suppose. I shall then begin at the old fountain with the aquatic monsters and the faun. If our meetings have taken place many times by the fountain, there is a certain likelihood that another one could occur in the same place. But if I am gliding in translucent nothingness, as I hope I am, Carolina could not be expecting me. Thus, she would have no reason to be at the fountain. Unless, of course, the fountain forms part of her private universe irrespective of me. Not knowing which of these instances is correct, I head toward the old fountain where, at a minimum, I will meet the faun.

My arrival at the fountain is a silent one. The only sound I hear is the splashing of water coming out of the faun's horn. Unlit as the fountain is and without a moon to reflect on its nervous water, the fountain is like a dark cave, a space that breathes but sheds no light. I am as unseen as the fountain is. And so is Carolina, for her presence, I cannot ascertain. So, I wait, bathing in the shadows and the silence.

I then hear the voice of a man and a woman approaching the fountain. I cannot elucidate what they say to each other. There is a quick and shallow laugh, perhaps a nervous laugh; then they stop talking. They come close to where I stand and ignore me completely. Eventually, they go past me. I do not exist for them; why should I? They are swallowed by the night, and

I remain alone and waiting. Would I find Carolina? Would she allow me to find her? I could talk to the faun and ask him if he has seen her. Would he answer? The faun, however, is concentrating on blowing his horn and cares not for my ruminations. But even if he were to answer, would I trust what he has to say?

It always happens that Carolina comes to meet me after I have been searching for her. She is the one who completes my search by making her presence a reality. I have yet to encounter her without me first beginning to search for her. How then could I know that she was not always there? She could be present, uninterruptedly, without me knowing. In that case, it is possible that she has never been absent. She does walk away and vanishes after we meet, but that may not necessarily mean that she has become absent, as I tend to think. Maybe I do not comprehend the full nature of her being.

The night is breathing peacefully. With no fixed duration, the night seems content to just be. It disregards my desires, for the night does not depend on me. I am in its womb, but the night does not know it. I could become peaceful like the night and care not for the duration of my search. Why worry? If the outcome of my search will be an encounter with Carolina, albeit not at a time of my choice, why should I be concerned with duration? It seems to me that the best approach is to expect nothing at any given moment in time.

The universe does not disappoint me. As I engage in the act of expecting nothing, nothing indeed happens. The faun keeps on blowing his horn, the passersby keep on passing, the night keeps on breathing, I keep on waiting, and Carolina keeps on not making her presence known. Nothing other than what is actually happening is happening. I take comfort in this experience because it feels soothing. I wonder, however, if by not expecting anything and simply residing under the night as a passive entity, I would be abandoning my intention to search for Carolina. And if my search is the catalyst for her eventual appearance, would I not be dismantling that potential appearance? An insult to myself, that would be.

Perhaps the answer is not in the search for an answer. If what happens, happens because nothing else could happen instead, then searching for Carolina or searching for the whereabouts of the crib of all waves and the burning star is futile. I should be content with the events as they occur, even if I cannot find an explanation for such occurrences. The problem is that the mind does not rest and demands an answer because it cannot ascertain the logic behind those absences. Logic travels in a linear direction and is intrinsically expectant. My mind, my very own mind, could be setting me up. By looking for logical explanations, it creates unfulfillable expectations, thus leading me to inevitable disappointments. Beware of the mind!

The night has no perfume of its own. The breath that I smell is a conglomerate of essences that reside under the veil of the night. I am one among those entities. There are others, but not many of them currently. The absence of a crowd may be responsible for the stillness of this night. I am alone with the faun and the monsters. We are all still. The only substance flowing is the water in the fountain which would prefer to be still but is instead propelled by a pump somewhere. Since nothing propels me, I decide to remain still.

The shadow of a man wearing a hat breaks the stillness of the night. It is an oblique shadow moving at a very slow pace. I cannot perceive the smell of the shadow. Maybe the shadow is not breathing. I cannot hear the steps responsible for moving the shadow either. At first, it seems to be moving away from me, but something makes it turn, and it then starts to move in my direction. I turn to stone. Motionless and soundless, I wait for the shadow to advance. It begins to grow as it cuts through the night and gets closer to me. Step-by-step, it creeps closer until it finally touches me. I feel nothing. I follow the shadow with my eyes to its physical source. The body casting the shadow has stopped its march completely and remains silent. I try to see the face of the man under the hat, but the dim light is shining from behind him his face. All I see is the dark side of a moon.

—I was looking for you.

—I cannot see your face. Who are you?

—Zotikos.

—Zotikos, I wasn't expecting to see you.

—You just said that you cannot see me.

—I see your shadow.

—That's not me.

—No, you are not your shadow. But your shadow owes itself to you.

—That's not my fault.

—But it is your consequence.

—An unintended consequence.

—Perhaps. But what's your intention in looking for me?

—I went by Café Central and didn't find you there. So, I left.

—Then, you weren't looking for me in this place.

—No, not by this fountain, but at Café Central.

—So, it is by chance that you find me here.

—You could say so.

—Well, now that you found me, for what purpose were you looking for me at Café Central?

—For the same purpose that I always look for you over there, for the sharing of nothingness.

Those words stay floating in the stillness of the night. I do not respond to them. Zotikos stays equally silent. I wonder if he truly believes that nothingness exists as a substance that can be shared. He treats it like an invaluable bounty. Perhaps he feels like nothingness is his dearest creation, his magnum opus. I will not know until I read what he has been writing.

Silently, his oblique shadow begins to pull away. It gradually loses its shape; it crumbles into the unanimous night. Nothing is left of Zotikos nor of his shadow.

#

Nothing in this universe is created anew. Matter is only transformed, not created nor destroyed. I believe the same happens with events and feelings. What we experience today is a mere representation of actions, gestures, and thoughts that have happened at another point in time. The same wars are fought over and over. Different warriors fight them, but they are the same wars. When friends meet and rejoice in their mutual company, it is friendship that re-emerges. Lovers make use of the love that has been present since the dawn of time. Homer already put his finger on all relevant aspects of the human condition. This may be the stage of our time, but the play has already been performed.

What I am now experiencing, these devastating absences, must have occurred to others in the past. And because others would have been impacted just as I am being impacted, an emotional response must be registered somewhere. I assume a writer would have felt the same need to work through the absences by means of his or her pen. I am not alone in this, and I am clearly not unique. There must be books containing thoughts and insights into this common experience. Even if those responses are not assembled in a singular and cohesive volume, elements must be scattered among all the books in the world. I just need to find them.

I stand in front of my bookshelves and look at a great many volumes arranged in no clear order. Some books matter to me more than others, but all could equally contain an emotional response to a perceived absence. Then there are the books I have never read, slumbering in other people's bookshelves and musty libraries all over the world. Those are more in number than the ones in front of me. Those are the shadows that my light cannot illuminate. But I can only touch that which I can reach.

I close my eyes and stretch my hand. With my fingers, I palpate the spines of various books and pick one without consciously choosing, as I have done in the past. I open the book and cover the top and bottom of the page with my hands to preserve the anonymity of its author. I read a random paragraph: *There is the music of birds and elephants. There is the music of fish underwater. There is the music of falling leaves. And there is the music of the world spinning and the winds whirling.* I do not remember reading those words, and I cannot identify the author. But there is a sense of yearning for a substance that cannot be apprehended. If music is not heard, is it absent or merely not existing? If we can conceive of an experience in a metaphorical way, does it become absent when reality fails to deliver a tangible version of it? Furthermore, when I see with my mind's eye, am I guaranteeing blindness in the prosaic but real world right in front of me?

I grab another book by lot. Given the thickness and weight of the book, I guess this is a compendium, poetry most likely. I take care not to peak at the title or any other revelatory information. When I crack the book open, I immediately see that the text is arranged in verses. Yes, this is poetry, but I do not know whose poetry it is. In the spirit of chance and serendipity, I read a single word from various random pages. The resulting phrase goes something like this: *your laugh eats sunrays, in golden seaweed.* I cannot believe what I am reading. The three-letter words I refuse to pronounce are thrust at me by this unknown poet, probably dead, who knows nothing about my reality. Those two elements are not actually discussed, but the words "rays" and "weed" pertain to them intimately. It is by association that the poet conjures that which is now missing in my world. I could do likewise; I could approach the absences I face by indirect means. Perhaps this is how Zotikos deals with his own dilemmas. His obliquity is not a chance operation.

I return the books to an empty space in the bookshelf and turn around without looking at the titles. They will remain as anonymous comrades, whisperers without body or face. I must now consider how to go to the shore without heading in that direction. How do I move through the shadows as if bathed by daylight? How to find Carolina without looking for her, and how to finish the manuscript by not writing another word? It is possible that those actions are only metaphors, that they represent the antithesis of what I truly want to do. But there is nothing wrong with alimenting those metaphors while real life is sorted out.

The first order of events will be a glass of pastis. Then I will try to forget that there are certain important elements missing in my life. I will not sit down to write until I reach the peaceful state of not caring, not caring where I come from and what has happened lately. What matters now is where I am going. And where I am going will not follow a predetermined trajectory. The words will have to write themselves out, the light will have to shine on itself, and life will have to live itself. Purpose will need to find another body to inhabit.

I begin to consider the possibility that the caravels will never make their return. Nobody has seen them in a very long time, and nobody may ever see them again. They have moved on in time, perhaps, or they have been dismantled and used as firewood. Something has changed, and that is why we do not see them anymore. If change is inevitable, why am I fighting it? If a tree is meant to grow, why trim its branches? Why try to stop the river from flowing? Why wish for light on this earth if darkness is inevitable at the end? Change is the only certainty I can count on. But when change happens, I find myself trying to unearth an explanation. An absence acquires its weight and significance commensurate with the degree of change it introduces in our lives. But if change is an intrinsic part of the universe, so may be the multiple absences. Perhaps absences are not that mysterious at all. They may be just as natural and expected as any change.

I could accept that this night is never going to end. If I were to do so, my life would acquire a completely different rhythm. Given sufficient time, I would adapt to that rhythm. The problem is that I will likely remember the light of day for as long as my memory remains intact. However, if I were to forget the illuminated part of my life, then an unending night would be just perfect. The impact of change is thus dependent on a healthy memory. And so is the case with any absence. They are felt for as long as we remember that which we no longer have. But could I force my mind to forget anything? If I succeeded in doing so, I could free myself. Probably not because in the act of selecting what to forget, I would be remembering the very thing I am trying to forget. So, forgetting must happen without effort, like gas molecules that grow apart and dissipate in the atmosphere. Accepting is not forgetting; it is learning to live with unexpected change.

I serve myself another glass of pastis and sit at my desk. Tonight, I will not write about the absences as I have been doing lately. Instead, I will assume that the world has been this way forever, that any changes that have occurred have been assimilated, that the way I now live is how I have always lived. I will not reminisce of my walks along the shore when I heard the seagulls and delighted myself looking at the immense blue above the sand. I will not confer daylight any superiority over darkness. I will not wish for Carolina to find me somewhere in the village. I fear, however, that I will be left with nothing to write about.

#

No, I am not the center of the universe. I perceive everything that is contained in the universe through my sense organs, and then my mind assigns order and meaning. But my mind is not the center of anything, for there is no center. I am inconsequential. I attach tremendous importance to the events that alter my life and come to consider those events as monumental as if they tilt the very axis on which the world spins. Does it really matter if the moon never gets to enjoy its reflection any longer? From my self-centered and minuscule private world, that seems like an atrocity. But, perhaps the moon does not care for its reflection or its position in relation to our spinning world. I am certain the moon does not care about me. We attract each other as any two bodies would according to the laws of physics, but that is an impersonal attraction. I used to hear the waves whispering while I walked down the shore. But they never spoke to me directly. They were preoccupied with their incessant comings and goings. Waves are probably being born elsewhere, I am sure. And as for the burning star, it is clearly consumed by its own heat and cares not for the destruction it will ensue once it arrives at its final burst. The heat the burning star emits does not come out of warmth.

Carolina is a different story. Like myself, she is inconsequential to the universe. However, two inconsequential beings can affect each other. I believe I exist for her in those isolated moments when we meet. But for each of us, that is a very small part of our personal universes. I am not the center of her universe, and she is clearly not the center of mine. But her absence is a hard one to endure, nonetheless. I felt sad when she did not materialize at the fountain the other night, or this night for it has not yet ended.

Not being at the center of anything implies that I am at the center of nothing. If I were to stretch my arms and touch what is around me, I would be touching pure nothingness. If nothing is what extends around me, any intentional motion on my part will bring me nowhere. The universe, not being around me, can only be contained within me, constituting my own center. No, I am not the center of the universe because the universe is the center of my very self. Everything that is there can be found inside myself. Outside, then, there is nothing.

Should I be so concerned about what happens in the universe? More precisely, should I be concerned about what happens inside of me? Inside of my chest, my heart beats, and my lungs absorb oxygen. But I cannot control how they do it. They are vital to me; however, I have never seen them. Likewise, I cannot alter or influence the course of the universe that resides inside of me. It operates on its own and responds not to my wishes. But I have a will, and that may suffice. It is my will and no one else's. The will, like the universe, is housed inside of me. I may decide to scream or stay silent, to open my eyes to the outside shadows or to close all windows, to turn to lead and be passive, or to revolve with exuberance. I can decide to collect the words I have already written and bring them to Zotikos or burn the manuscript in the fireplace. There are no forces opposing my will, at least none that I am aware of. Whatever happens in the universe simply happens. It is up to me to mount a response.

My first decision is to stop writing immediately. The phrases that I have been weaving must contain all the necessary meanings to approximate an understanding of all possible absences. The literary work is something like an arena in which the reader and author participate in a game of the imagination. I have started and completed my phase of the creative process. Zotikos would need to finish his own phase. He has been playing along, imagining, evading, and writing as well. I will read his manuscript and he will read mine, thus completing the circle. Whether a full picture of our changing universe will emerge, I cannot predict with certainty.

I will venture out into the streets once more. If I were to rest trapped inside my apartment, the universe inside of me would continue to change without impacting any other universe. It is in the mingling of individual universes that our very own universe finds its meaning. It may not matter who crosses my path and what influences result from those encounters. If I come across Carolina, the better. If I do not, so be it. I do have a will, but I cannot *will* any event into existence.

When I look at the rooms comprising my apartment and at the objects filling those rooms, I feel small. How small the world around me! How insignificant! I could introduce change by rearranging the furniture and moving pictures around, but to what avail? It would be like ushering in insignificance by means of variation. Clearly, the real amplitude is the one found inside of me. And that amplitude goes wherever I go.

I gather my manuscript and hold it together with a simple rubber band. That is sufficient. I then pour myself a small glass of pastis and sit down for a moment. I have integrated all I could from the experiences forced upon me, and I have given them form and meaning through the process of writing. However, when I try to recollect the story I have been writing, my mind offers no images. Yes, I am holding the text with my own hands, and I can feel the weight of the pages, but nothing forms in my mind's eye. The game of the imagination has ended for me.

#

I storm out of my apartment with my manuscript held tightly. We are one and the other. The words form the manuscript, but I sourced the words. The manuscript has formed me in the process of me writing it. The imagination has intervened in the formation of my ideas. But the imagination needs words to come into existence. Likewise, my ideas cannot exist without words. The manuscript needs my words as well, but I need the words to think. We are each an extension of the other, the manuscript and me.

The streets accept me with the same indifference as ever. Whether day or nighttime, my walking around is largely irrelevant. The shadows embrace me because they have no other choice. They are so numerous and seem to get bored when not engulfing people. I disregard the sense of insignificance and continue to walk through the absence of light. Nothing guides my steps, for there is no agency in my walking other than offering my universe a release. I breathe in the loose air to bring the outside universe into mine. And with each exhalation, part of my inner universe is released. The intermingling of universes is certain to happen.

It occurs to me that by willingly rejecting an impulse to choose, a sort of choice is being made in the process. It may be impossible to walk nowhere because I am effectively moving forward with every step I take, and forward is already a direction. Alternatively, I could walk without agency if I do not direct my steps away from any specific destination. Rejecting is not the choice that I want to make at this moment. My unbridled steps move me through the village and, soon enough, I find myself in the vicinity of Café Central. Could it be an instinctual process that guides me here, or perhaps a pattern ingrained in my muscle memory, or maybe the attractive forces of other universes? I cannot be certain what the reasons are, but I will not fight against them.

Turning around a familiar corner brings me in full view of Café Central. The place is rather busy, which means this must be around the middle of the workday. The chandeliers are lit, but there is not enough light for me to identify people's faces. What is clear is that someone is sitting at my table, a woman, it seems. I could turn around and walk away without inquiring any further. But what is there to fear? If someone else has acquired the habit of sitting at my table in my absence, then that person is unknowingly attracted to my universe. That would only be natural and not dangerous. Either by willful decision or by a deep-rooted habit, I move closer and closer until I can distinguish the faces of people at Café Central. There is Maurice, brisk as usual, moving from one customer to the next. And at my table, sitting completely alone, I recognize Carolina's face.

Am I finding Carolina without her finding me first? None of our fortuitous meetings have ever taken place at Café Central. This is where I exist, at that very table where she is now sitting. Is she existing there on her own, in my absence? Maybe she knows that I am walking in that direction and is simply waiting for my arrival. But I did not plan to go anywhere in particular. I am here due to unclear forces. She could not have determined in advance what those forces are. In essence, it is highly improbable that she is waiting for me. And if she is not awaiting me, it follows that she exists at my very table without considering my presence.

If I approach her, an encounter will take place. This one is certainly not a planned one. Or is it? Maybe this meeting is as planned as the other seemingly unplanned ones. Perhaps we have never had random encounters at all. What if every encounter, either at the bridge or by the fountain, have been perfectly orchestrated by Carolina? If so, then she has never been absent. She would have had full knowledge of my whereabouts, my walks, even my writing habits. What appears like an absence every time she vanishes away, leaving me alone, could have been only a retreat, while the essence of her presence still lingers in the air. But I have not smelled that essence. Or maybe I lack the capacity to sustain her constancy, to remember her perfume.

Today I am choosing not to reject, not to walk away. So, I make my way to Café Central and sit at my table opposite Carolina. She does not seem surprised to see me. Her expression is calm and content at the same time. She does not greet me. She looks at me as if I had always been here in front of her. My arrival has not changed the flow of her reality. For my part, I feel like she has been completely absent since we last saw each other in my apartment. For her, though, it seems like I have never gone away. I cannot understand how this discrepancy comes about, but it is palpable to me. For fear of shattering this moment of tranquility, I stay quiet. Carolina has no need for quietness and begins talking at once.

—That must be your manuscript. Have you finished it?

—I'm done with the game of imagination.

—Marvelous! So what game are you going to play next?

—The game of reality, maybe…

—That's a hard game to play, don't you think?

—It seems increasingly so. If there are rules for that game, nobody knows what they are. And nobody knows who the real players are.

—Yes, it is a hard game. But you don't have to play it. I don't.

—Maybe I should write about reality to understand it better.

—You wrote this a book about what's not there. Now you propose to write another book about what's there for real.

—What's there for real is my entire universe, everything that's inside of me. It is less questionable than what's outside.

—Be careful, the two books could cancel each other out, and you may be left with nothing.

—Yes, nothingness seems to be more and more abundant.

—But you don't have to fear it. Look at me; I don't.

No, she does not. She is calm and content, and her world appears to be rather complete. She does not appear to have needs outside of what the moment provides for her. Every moment is full and continuous, with all other moments that are full as well. Everything is eternally present for her. That may be why I am always there, next to her, even when I am not. I may have been mistaken when thinking that I cease to exist the moment she vanishes away. It is she who vanishes away from my universe, not the opposite. I may be ever-present, for Carolina at least.

—Where are you going with your manuscript?

—I'm not sure. To the streets, to the market, to the shore, everywhere, nowhere…

—Those are all wonderful places. And what will you

do when you get there?

—I'll hand the manuscript to someone. Even though I'm done with the game of imagination, the manuscript is incomplete. It needs to find its doppelgänger.

—Why don't you give it to me? I'll be happy to read it.

—Because I'm not sure that I'll ever see you again.

—We cannot be sure of anything.

—You're right. But I can only tolerate so many absences. You vanish often, and if the manuscript vanishes with you, then I'll have nothing.

Carolina does not reply. She offers me a smile, the tender smile of one who understands. Does she understand that this night is never-ending and that the shore surrounds a vast desert where the blue body of water used to rest? Does she understand that if the moon does not see its own reflection, it will cease to recognize itself? Does she understand that when she vanishes, I am left hurting? Maybe she does.

My first consideration is to remain at the table and contemplate Carolina's smile until this night finally comes to an end. But as she just said, we cannot be sure of anything. The burning star may emerge from behind the eastern hills in the next minute or in the next century. Or it may never ever emerge. I cannot tell. Likewise, Carolina may remain seated across from me, holding her placid smile, or she may just get up, walk away, and vanish once more. All these expectations are void and promise nothing. And nothing is beginning to occupy a rather large part of my universe.

I rest not. I need to continue my movement, turning and turning, until my inner universe loses all consequences. I get on my feet and hold on to my manuscript. I look at Carolina and wonder if we would ever encounter each other again. I turn my back and walk away from my table, from Café Central, into the streets, into the night. I vanish.

#

As I wander through the streets, I begin to question whether my expectations have a rational base. The absences that have occurred have severely impacted my psyche, and I have written about them to come to terms with the entire experience. What else could I have done? My words are the only tool at my disposal.

Those words come from inside myself, where my personal universe resides. But because of writing about the absences, I have created an unsustainable expectation: somehow, my reality will revert to what it used to be. I may search everywhere, but I doubt there is a rational base for that expectation. The temptation is to reject that expectation for lack of substantiality. But I have agreed not to reject anything. Thus, I wander and wonder.

Let the breeze come to meet me, let the sounds of the village surround me. Let the waters of the fountain sing, let the faun blow his horn. Let the hours slip by, let me integrate everything that comes my way. Let my inner universe mingle with all other universes. Let me expect nothing by accepting everything. The night is the night, and the desert at the shore is the desert. The words that I have spun to describe them are the words. Everything is what it is and nothing else.

My steps take me where they may. I do not guide them, nor do I oppose them. I allow them to float, and I float along with them. The village passes by me, and I recognize many corners, many alleys. Other unfamiliar ambits welcome my passage. I flow unencumbered, unattached, essentially free. I cannot tell where I am going, but I am going. And this is the way because the way is the way.

The breeze gathers some velocity and becomes the wind. It does not push me back, nor does it usher me along. It is just a stronger presence, the wind, and I welcome its force. The battle between the light of the lampposts and that of the stars has not subsided. But ahead of me, a territory opens where the stars seem to dominate. They appear free to shine unopposed by sublunar lights. As I wander in that direction, all sounds begin to vanish, one by one, until a magnanimous silence installs itself all around me. I realize I have arrived at the shore without wanting, or the shore has come to greet me. The long shore lies on its back and looks up at the moonless night. It curves naturally as it hugs the land on one side while giving a wide berth to the absence on the other side. I doubt that the shore has expectations of witnessing the birth of waves once again or the purported return of the caravels. The shore is the shore and nothing else.

The silence slows me down; it permits me to contemplate the vastness of the night and the emptiness facing me. In the absence of seagulls and waves, the silence grows and becomes a universe, a seemingly empty universe. I do not hear my steps, nor do I hear the wind battering the world. All I hear is the flow of blood through my veins and the low hum of my thoughts inside my mind. This is a generous silence; it allows me to exist free from interferences so I can find more of myself. By taking away the extraneous, the silence gives abundantly.

I could search for a reason explaining my arrival at the silent shore. A futile search that would be, since I gave free reign to my feet and imposed no agenda. I am here now, by chance, by need, pushed by forces unknown to me, or perhaps because the gravitational force of another universe is attracting mine. I cannot tell, and it does not matter. What counts is that I am here, and my manuscript is with me. What will happen next is of no consequence at this very moment. So, I turn to the contemplation of the void before my eyes and listen to the resonant silence.

Directly behind me, a window opens, and light begins to emanate from it. It is a yellow light, one that has been incarcerated. Suddenly, the silhouette of a man interrupts the flow of light. It does not block the light completely, but it deforms its flow. The window is on the third floor of a building I believe I recognize. The man, his face obscure, must be Zotikos, who is looking out into the night, possibly searching for words or the absent moon. He cannot imagine that I am looking at his silhouette; neither could I have predicted that I would be standing here looking at him. But things are what they are, and events turn out as they may. For that very reason, I will make my presence known to Zotikos.

I let myself into the building and climb up to the third floor. Once in the hallway, I am confronted with three doors, all closed and indistinctive. I could knock on every single one of them, or I could choose one. Choosing is a form of rejection, so I decide not to choose. Since this is the third floor, I decide to knock on the third door from the left, thus keeping a sense of symmetry. I knock on the door—Zotikos answers.

—What a surprise! I could've never imagined you knocking at my door. How did you find where I live?

—I could've never imagined this was your door. In fact, I didn't find you.

—That's perfect, then. Please come in.

The incarcerated yellow light is everywhere. It bounces from wall to wall and gives the place a musty appearance. Zotikos shows me to a small table and invites me to have a seat. He then disappears to what must be a sort of kitchen and then comes back with two glasses topped with ice, a bottle of pastis, and some water. Without asking, he prepares the drinks. He then says nothing more, and I reciprocate by staying quiet. From where I am sitting, I can see the open window and the darkness outside. I wonder what Zotikos sees when he looks out that window. I wonder if he would admit that there is an incredible void outside.

I place my manuscript on top of the table and continue to nurse my silence. Zotikos looks at the manuscript but does not reach for it. Instead, he drinks a mouthful of pastis and disappears into another room untouched by the yellow light. When he returns, he has brought a manuscript with him and places it next to mine on the table. There they are, two parallel lines approaching each other, perhaps related, or perhaps not related at all. Not different from the relationship between the two of us. Here I am, sitting next to Zotikos while we relate to each other only obliquely.

The manuscripts remain unopened, and Zotikos and I remain silent. I am a stranger in a strange place across from an evident absence that defies verification. A most unnatural situation this is, but the situation at hand at this moment. I sip some of my pastis and prepare to endure a long silence. I realize I have no control over the circumstances, but I am content to accept them as they are. Our divergent paths have coalesced multiple times, bringing us together. This is not different; this is just how universes mingle.

After a long while, Zotikos gets up from the table and walks over to the open window. He stands there looking outside. The economy of his gestures tells me he is not surprised by the darkness or the abundant silence. He seems to be looking at a familiar scenario where everything seems to be where it has always been. He then closes the window and returns to the table. He prepares a second round of drinks and places his hand on top of my manuscript.

—I believe this is for me to read.

—It's inevitable, the confluence of the streams.

—I understand. Then take this manuscript of mine

and do unto it as I'll do unto yours.

—Fine, we'll bring our joint book into existence.

What follows next is silence, for we each understand that the spoken word is superfluous at this moment. What needed to be said has already been said. What needed to be written has already been written. We now need to accumulate our respective souls in the process of reading each other's manuscript. One reality will inform and form the other, and vice versa. My inner universe will accommodate his. Thus, the creative process will be completed. And Zotikos will do likewise.

We take the necessary time to finish what is left of the pastis. Rituals need completion if they are to be effective. By now, it is clear that I must continue the march that brought me to this place. The yellow light has shinned over this encounter and will rest a witness to our agreement. I then get up from the table and grab Zotikos' manuscript. I leave mine behind and head for the door.

#

The unending night, the void, the breeze wanting

salt, the absence of the burning star, the absence of the crib of all waves... All confront me at once when I step away from Zotikos' place and come to stand at the shore. These entities have become inconveniently familiar, and I have no control over them. What is unfamiliar to me is the manuscript I took from Zotikos. I cannot imagine what it contains nor how it is written. He said he was writing about nothing, but I do not really know what nothing means to him. However, I do have control over the manuscript. I can read it and bring it to life.

I leave the street behind me and descend unto the vast deserted seabed. If I were to continue walking, would I reach other lands? Would those lands be under a cloak of darkness? Would people in those lands see the universe as I see it? It does not matter, for I have no control over anything. Thus, I accept the peace of the moment and lie on my back to contemplate the moonless night.

All the nights, the night. All the silences, the silence. The universe inside of me has the same profundity as the night, as the silence. There is no absence in my universe because it has gained its presence once an absence is perceived. I touch the sand under my back, and it is present. I reach out with my hand and touch the air; it is also present. I feel the manuscript, and it is certainly present. Everything is present and occupies a space in my inner universe. Nothingness is also there, a fluid and penetrating substance.

Suddenly, a sound the likes of which I have never heard before reaches my ears like a faint humming that comes from no clear source. It is not an animal sound, nor is it a voice. The sound begins to evolve gradually by gathering deeper tones and undertones. It reverberates in the darkness. The sound grows slowly and starts to replace the silence of the night. The aural space is no longer empty; it now contains vibrations. Not only do I hear this sound, but I can feel its pressure on my chest. As I lie still, the sound engulfs me and makes its presence known. But abruptly, the universe becomes quiet again. The silence establishes itself once more. However, this silence is a nervous one. It is the silence of annunciation. Then I hear the breaking of bells, the whirling of the earth, the howling of mad winds, the thunderous rupture of the night. And with it comes a white light that floods everything, revealing in its wake what the night had absconded. It then shows its face to me—the moon.

The star is burning again. On the other side of the earth, the sun has re-emerged in all its rage. I cannot see it from where I am, but the face of the moon does not lie. This heralds the end of the unending night. This turns an absence into a definitive presence. I do not know what led to the absence, nor what brought it to an end. What seems evident is that dawn will come to meet me soon enough. I accept this rapture even though I cannot decipher its nature.

This is a pure moonlight, nubile and immaculate. But without a mirror, the moon cannot admire its own beauty. It will need to wait for the return of the caravels to be able to contemplate its face again. This moonlight puts into evidence the vast desert in front of me. It extends as far as the white light shines, and at the very end, the desert seems to curve at the edges before vanishing. I cherish this light. I bathe in it.

Under the immaculate moonlight, the pages of Zotikos' manuscript acquire the appearance of pale flesh: pure and inviting. I will start reading the manuscript now. I will bring it into life under this unexpected light.

It seems only natural for the universe to enlace the rebirth of light with the birth of the book. Whether the moonlight will last enough time for me to finish the manuscript, I cannot tell. How long would it take for dawn to arrive? I know not.

The first page of the manuscript is completely blank; not a single word is printed on it. The white page reflects the pure light coming from the moon's face, a face that reflects the ardent light from the nascent sun whose face is not yet visible. The blank page emits a radiant nothingness, both beautiful and profound. When I contemplate this page, I think of Zotikos and the yellow light that infiltrates his apartment. He knows about this other light, the lunar one, and he wanted to share it with me. The next page is as blank as the first one, but it reflects the moonlight in a different way. It bestows it with a certain warmth. Perhaps the result of refraction, that oblique passing of the light through the mediums. Or maybe it is my interpretation of the light that gives it a different hue. The next page, equally blank, makes me shiver. Not because of the absence of printed words but because of the pearlescence of the reflected light.

With the turning of the pages comes the passing of

time, and with the passing of time comes the transmutation of moonlight into emotions—the slow accumulation of the soul of the other. And so, I proceed, through all the pages, through the hours, deciphering a universe composed of intangibles. As I bring life to Zotikos' blank manuscript, the nothingness he struggled with finds a place inside my inner universe. I integrate his perceived absences, and I am the better for it.

Time, moonlight, time, the soul, time, nothingness, time, the universe—over and over. Then, a misty brightness gently tears the cloak of night. Dubitative at first, but an unrelenting brightness. It begins to push against the night sky; it boils with ambition. This brightness frames the vast absence in front of me; it demarcates its contours. I marvel at the miracle. I can now distinguish the curvature of the absence far in the horizon, and it fills me with pleasure. Dawn arrives gradually, and her carriage drags along a burning sun—a sun that burns as intense as the one that had gone missing.

I lie on my back and allow for the newly born morning to enter my inner universe. It quickly finds a place to rest, tucked inside an empty room where the absence of the sun used to repose. The room next to it is still occupied by the absence of the blue above the sand. I wonder if that room will be vacated as well. Then a warm breeze blows inland. It seems to come from the radiant horizon and is redolent of saltpeter. And sustained by that breeze comes a flock of seagulls, mewing and laughing. These are imminent signs that my reality is changing. But I know that things are what they are and nothing more. So, I reject nothing; I accept everything—I am inconsequential.

First, there is a wetness, then the foam, then the licking of a timid wave. The sea rising, submerging the desert, ushering a blue that extends as far as I can see. There, where the curve of the horizon separates the nubile sea from the morning sky, the sails of the caravels flutter in the breeze. I swim toward them.

www.ingramcontent.com/pod-product-compliance
Lightning Source LLC
Chambersburg PA
CBHW011322310726
48973CB00011B/3021